FIRE
BREAK

Jennifer Phillips

Book design by Karli Kruse
Cover design by Karli Kruse
Cover photographs by Shutterstock Images

Published in the United States by Jolly Fish Press, an imprint of North Star Editions, Inc.

This is a work of fiction. Names, characters, places, and incidents are either the product of the author's imagination or are used fictitiously, and any resemblance to actual persons living or dead, business establishments, events, or locales is entirely coincidental.

Library of Congress Cataloging-in-Publication Data (pending)
978-1-63163-841-1 (paperback)
978-1-63163-840-4 (hardcover)

Jolly Fish Press
North Star Editions, Inc.
2297 Waters Drive
Mendota Heights, MN 55120
www.jollyfishpress.com

Printed in the United States of America

FIRE BREAK

Jennifer Phillips

JOLLY
FiSH
PRESS
Mendota Heights, Minnesota

CHAPTER 1

I replayed the final point in my head while I headed off the court. I'd tried to rally. But my mind hadn't been on the game. And my reflexes had been toast. One lightning-fast serve, and my opponent had taken me out in record time.

WHACK.

I banged my racket down harder on the bench than I'd intended. That probably confused my teammates even more than my awful match. *So unlike Alia*. That's what they would say about me after I left.

But the lecture I dreaded never came. A gentle hand touched my shoulder. The understanding look of my tennis coach made it somehow worse. I tried apologizing. He just waved me toward the locker room.

A voice message waited on my phone.

"Alia, darling. I am so sorry I missed your match today. It was not planned, or I would have let you know. There is nothing wrong. Don't worry about me. I will explain tonight."

I replayed Oma's message. My grandma's voice soothed me with its soft German accent. She did sound okay. Still, my body tensed with worry. Why didn't she explain what happened?

My phone buzzed with a text: *Waiting*. I skipped the shower and didn't bother changing into street clothes. I needed to leave this day behind.

Melissa was sprawled on the stairs outside the sports complex. We made an odd pair. I always looked like I'd just left the gym. Melissa looked like she'd raided a costume sale. She dressed and carried herself like the curtain was going up any moment. Today, she wore an old-fashioned dress from the 1800s, a hat with netting over her eyes, and makeup meant to stand out under bright lights. Usually, she gave me a hard time about how long she had to wait for me. It didn't matter how long she'd *actually* waited. Today, I just got a pity look.

"You saw my message," I confirmed. I'd sent it after my meeting with the principal this morning.

She nodded. We walked our usual shortcut toward the town's main street. Above us, birds chattered their spring songs.

I took deep breaths until I could talk without bursting into tears. "I can't lose my sports privileges. And Oma didn't show this afternoon. She never misses my matches. I tanked."

Melissa's questions rushed at me like a mudslide. "What happened!? Was she in an accident? Is she okay?"

"She's fine, apparently. What a day."

"Well, the school is letting you finish this season. And I can't believe they'd yank you from tennis next year," Melissa said. "But I just don't get it. You have such laser concentration during games. Why not use that with your schoolwork? You need a new plan for studying."

My bitter laugh surprised even me. "No laser focus today. Not with worrying about Oma and school. And forget it. I don't need any more reading tricks. The whole thing is exhausting."

Melissa groaned. "You can't give up."

I gave her a look making it clear I already had.

"Take me through the meeting," she insisted.

I filled her in on the day's news. Looming academic probation. It was supposed to make me more motivated.

"Athletics alone won't get me through life," I said, copying the principal. "Like I don't know that. I wish people would accept I'm dumb."

Melissa threw her arm in front of me like a railroad crossing gate, stopping me cold. "Dramatics are my thing, so cut it out. You're not dumb. I thought kids with IEPs got a free pass. Isn't it illegal or something to kick you out of sports?"

"Individualized Education Programs aren't a free pass," I said. "They just put things in place to help you with class and homework. Besides, my parents are the ones insisting on it."

That thought smacked me in the face. My own parents

didn't understand how pointless all of the "interventions" were for me. They didn't think I tried hard enough. Now they and the school were threatening to take away the one thing I was actually good at.

For the last couple of blocks, we let the birds do the talking. Then we both stared at my driveway. Oma's car was missing. We'd expected her to be there, waiting for me to get home.

Melissa nodded toward my phone.

I checked and shook my head. No new messages. My gut felt like it had taken a karate kick.

Melissa rubbed my arm. "Take a shower. Recharge. And call me the micro-second you hear from Oma."

CHAPTER 2

Mom and Dad's strange behavior did nothing to calm my worries. They barely asked me about my match. They didn't bring up school. And they gave only a vague answer about Oma's absence. A doctor's appointment, that's all. No big deal. Something she couldn't schedule at a different time.

Right. Oma *always* scheduled her life around our events. She hadn't missed one of my matches in ten years.

After dinner, I disappeared to my room to study. I kept my space plain and neat. No distractions. Everything in its place.

Again and again, I tried forcing my eyes onto my homework. But the words danced around and refused to sit still. Even my usual tunes weren't helping me track the information. I crumpled up my attempts at handwritten notes and batted them across the room with my racket.

Ugh. The quiz. How was I going to get through that?

A faint vanilla scent wafted into the room. I turned around, heart lifting at the sight of Oma.

"I am so sorry I had to miss your match," she said. "I know your parents told you about my doctor's appointment."

"They didn't say what it was about. Or why it happened last minute. The truth, Oma. What gives?" She was a tiny little thing, but she wasn't frail or sickly.

"I had to go. They insisted."

"Who? Mom and Dad?"

Oma stayed quiet for a long moment.

"What?" I fought down a twinge of fear. "Are you sick? What's wrong?"

"The government," she said. "I thought I could escape their silly rule about getting a body scan and other tests after turning eighty. But they were going to cut off my benefits if I didn't comply."

I didn't know what she was talking about. But I didn't want her to worry. "If they took away your benefits, you could move in with us."

Oma ran her fingers through my hair. All my life, she had played with it and pinned it in place before my sports events. She liked to fake-complain about "this long, wild hair."

"No, my girl. I'm doing fine on my own. Going to this appointment was my one compromise to their never-ending rules."

Her words came out intense. That shook my insides. Oma didn't talk like this.

"I was scared," I said. "I thought you'd had an accident or something."

"I'm sorry. They decided to give me an escort to the appointment. I wasn't allowed to message anyone." She waved away my frown. "It's all done. I'm in compliance. And I will watch a replay of your match."

"Don't bother. I did awful today. It's not worth watching. It hasn't been a great day for me either."

"I'm sorry if my absence influenced your playing. But one game does not decide your future."

Her absence affected me more than I thought it would.

But it really wasn't her fault. Guilt-tripping her wouldn't do any good.

She spied a new bracelet on my nightstand and held it up to study. "I have a beautiful handmade silver bracelet I picked up in a market in Nepal. It will be yours when I'm eventually gone."

Oma liked to talk about her countless travels. I liked to listen. But I always ignored it when she talked about what would happen when she died. Why did old people do that? It made me think of something I didn't want to accept. That someday, she would be gone. She was my rock. She helped me figure out my life. I couldn't do that without her.

"Want to talk about the game?" she asked.

"Nope. I'm getting in the study zone right now." I refused to meet her gaze.

She kissed the top of my head and moved to the door.

"Oma!" I called out.

She waited.

"I'm glad you're okay. Will they keep hassling you?"

She gave me a tired smile. "Not if I can help it. Good night, sweet girl."

I returned to the quiz.

"Music up," I told my voice activation program.

The driving beat snapped my brain into high gear. Some people used soft music to help them concentrate. Not me.

"Oh my god! She's actually studying!" The squeaky voice of my seventh-grade brother broke my focus.

"Music down!" I grumbled, then gave Wally my best irritated look. "I study every night. Bug off. I'm busy. And you didn't knock. That's a quarter."

Wally sighed. "Later. I'm looking for my globe."

My brother wore his typical sports shirt uniform. Tonight, it was the Notre Dame Fighting Irish. His ongoing mission was to look athletic. It was a hard sell.

"I don't have your globe. Bye."

"Dad wants to know what you're working on." Wally savored carrying messages from our parents checking to make sure I was studying. On generous nights, I let him carry back the answer.

"I'll tell him. Buh-bye."

Wally rolled his eyes and left without another word.

"Music up," I said.

The song jogged my memory about one of my tutor's ideas. She suggested I try chanting or singing words while I read something hard. Why not?

Miracle of miracles, it got me through the quiz.

But then my thoughts locked back on to my problem. As a junior, I already had a decision looming about what I'd do after high school. Try going to college, or try going pro? Both meant I couldn't lose my sports.

I needed a game plan to show everyone I was seriously trying with schoolwork. Time to think of a strategy.

CHAPTER 3

In the morning, I tried to speed through breakfast. Yesterday still felt raw.

I ignored my mom's greeting and grabbed fixings for my smoothie. Wally shoveled in his food while reading a book. Hard to tell if Mom had already given him his morning hair ruffle. It always looked messed up beyond repair. Today he was pretending to be a soccer jock.

Dad tried saying something to me over the whirl of the blender. I turned it off.

"Did you finish your homework last night? I never got a report on what you were doing." He held up his coffee for a sip.

I took a deep breath. "Yep. Finished *two* assignments."

Dad shot Mom a pleased look of surprise. I took another deep breath.

My phone buzzed. My friends were already at the coffee shop.

"Let's get moving," I told Wally.

"I'll see you at today's match," Mom said. "I know yesterday was rough. But we'll be there today, okay?"

I forced out a little smile. If I talked, too much emotion would spill out. I gave Wally a ten-minute sign and dashed upstairs to finish getting ready for school.

He was pulling weeds in the front yard when I came down. Wally seemed to have Mom's green thumb.

"Let's rock. Let's roll," he muttered. We moved through the jungle of plants and hanging flowers to the sidewalk.

Wally and I didn't talk much on our walks to school. We liked to be off in our own worlds, thinking about things or listening to music. It's not that we didn't like each other. We just didn't feel the need to babble on.

I flicked him lightly on the head when we reached his school and dodged him trying to flick me back. Then I made a sharp right to walk the couple of blocks to the main drag.

I adjusted my backpack so my racket stopped smacking me in the back of my head and doubled my pace.

The smell of coffee pulled me into the Daily Shot coffee shop. The hissing of the milk steamer greeted me. I found Melissa and Jonah perched on the same stools they perched on every school morning. A third stool waited for me.

"We've got ten minutes," Jonah declared. "I have some rounds to make before class."

Melissa and I shared a smile. Jonah was our leader-of-the-future friend. Member of student council. Participant in DECA. Chair of his tribal youth board. And on and on.

"You're always making rounds, talking with people and making connections." I tugged on his ponytail while I took my usual spot.

"There are leaders, and there are followers," he replied. His large brown eyes sparkled with humor. "I know what I am. What are you?"

"Follower," I announced.

"Follower, and proud of it," Melissa agreed.

"As I thought. Then I will be your leader," Jonah said.

"We should have dumped him in the second grade," Melissa stage-whispered to me. Today's outfit included rainbow eye shadow and purple lips.

"Too late?" I stage-whispered back.

Jonah passed me my tall scalded milk from the barista. "I only tolerate you two so I can practice on you," he teased.

I rolled my eyes, then said, "New topic. I need your help."

They swiveled around to give me their attention.

"I've thought a lot about what I can do to not lose my sports. I'll try harder to pay attention. Try the million strategies they've taught me. Do the best I can. It won't actually help, but I'll make sure they see how I'm trying. What do you think?"

"You should speak up more. Pepper the teachers with lots of questions. Show them you want their help," Melissa suggested.

"And don't take this the wrong way," Jonah said. "But watch how your face looks in class."

"What?!" I blurted out. Melissa slapped his arm.

"Not my best choice of words," he said with a laugh. "What I mean is that sometimes you look really bored. Or like you're feeling lost. It doesn't help your cause."

He spoke the truth, even if I didn't like hearing it.

Jonah downed the last of his coffee and marched out the door. We obediently followed. It had been like this since we were pint-sized. Jonah in the lead, Melissa and I happily bringing up the rear. He just always knew where he wanted to go. We either didn't know or didn't care.

Normally, I walked this route to school on autopilot. I moved down the streets and turned corners without thinking. But this time, I noticed our route took us past the courthouse. Retired people liked to hang out there and do whatever retired folks liked to do. Some sat around talking. Others played board games like chess or checkers. I wondered if they were going through the same medical tests as Oma.

At school, I shoved Jonah and Melissa good-naturedly. Then I peeled off to the gym to stow my tennis gear. My stomach got that nervous squeeze that came every time I walked these halls.

School was so hard. And the truth was, Jonah was right. I thought most of the things being taught *were* boring. Or else I really did feel lost and unsure of what to say or ask. But my teachers and parents didn't want to hear that.

So, okay then. Game on.

CHAPTER 4

Hours later, I had a tennis victory under my belt as Mom and Oma cheered me on. But I also had a reminder from my IEP manager about missing assignments. My parents would see this on my student dashboard.

So, I hid in my bedroom to work on my World History homework. It was a perfect spring evening for a run. But I needed something to show when Mom and Dad confronted me about my assignments.

This homework was about genocide. Mr. Carver called it "trying to destroy a group of people, usually because of their heritage or way of life." For the assignment, we needed to write about whether the examples matched the definition of genocide. Analysis. Mr. Carver wanted to see our analysis.

I ran into problems quickly.

The pictures in our packet made my pulse race and my stomach cramp. Dead bodies. Faces filled with fear and anguish. Families forced into small, dirty spaces. Angry people. Hateful people.

And the complicated sentences stretched on, page after page after page. Too much text. Too many big words. Too many hard-to-get ideas. I paced my room, trying not to cry. How would any of my study strategies help with this?

Impossible.

The tears won. Game over.

What a perfect moment for Oma to appear.

"I knew you'd make a comeback today," she said. She held out her hand for a high five, then saw how upset I was. "What's wrong?"

"World History. Genocide," I blubbered. "I can't do this."

She tsked while she looked through the disturbing images. She landed on pictures from the Holocaust. Crap. I totally spaced.

"Sorry, Oma. I forgot."

"No worries. My German pride doesn't include making excuses. It's definitely a serious subject. We can't ignore it, even if it scares us deeply."

"But this is too much," I said. "Why is this class required anyway?"

"History teaches us that past events affect us even now. Don't forget Indigenous peoples in the United States. Genocide happened right here, on this soil. I know it feels like a million years ago. But Jonah lives with the effects of that today."

I couldn't begin to connect the dots between this subject and one of my best friends. Oma had to be stretching things to make a point.

She looked at my assignment sheet. It listed early warning signs that a group was being targeted for oppression. Oma seemed to be debating something in her head.

"What?" I prodded her.

"I think it would be good for you to consider things happening right now. With people my age. Right under your nose. You might find more connections than you realize."

"Seriously?" A laugh escaped me. Then I choked it down, seeing the look on her face. "What?"

She took time with her words. "Why do I have to get medical tests I don't want? Why must people leave their homes and—" She shook her head and eyed me sternly. "I need to take off. I have a meeting. But come out from your teen universe for a bit. We'll talk more later."

She turned toward the doorway.

"Wait! I didn't see anything listed," I said. Oma was such a part of our daily lives that she added her appointments to our family calendar app.

She didn't answer before she disappeared out the door.

In her absence, pieces of family conversations rushed into my head. So did comments I'd heard at school or around the neighborhood. Things I'd ignored or never really tried to understand.

Worries about too many people in the country growing old. Not enough money to care for everyone. Some young people getting irritated, calling old folks a burden. News reports about old people being attacked.

Looking back, it was a big deal when Oma turned eighty. Hushed discussions between my parents stopped when Wally or I came into the room. And Oma missed my match to go to the doctor. Something the government forced her to do.

Oma wanted me to think about old people and genocide? Maybe something wrong was happening. That seemed way out there. But still, I decided to go through the early warning signs. I could tell Oma I did it. She'd tell Mom and Dad. That would be a point in my favor on the homework front.

I ran my finger down the list.

A group is targeted and isolated. Maybe? I wasn't sure about the isolated part. But it seemed like their age was making old people a target.

Civil rights are limited. I'd have to look that up later.

An atmosphere of hatred builds up. Possible. Resentment

seemed to be growing about having to take care of old people.

The group's property is destroyed. I didn't know.

Members of the group suffer attacks. Sounded like it.

Derogatory slogans and names become commonplace. I searched online and learned *derogatory* meant *insulting*. Nothing that I knew about. Still, I hadn't been paying attention.

I didn't know what to think about the rest of the signs. It didn't matter. Terrifying thoughts filled my head.

This was too much. I tried getting a grip. My grandma couldn't really be in danger. This assignment was spooking me. She was exaggerating. It was a trick to get me to study more. That must be what she was doing.

I finished the homework and got ready for bed. But thoughts about hate and doom pressed down on me. I couldn't unwind. My mind kept racing. I'd call Oma in the morning to see how serious she was. Hopefully she'd fess up to trying to help me focus while studying.

CHAPTER 5

I left my window cracked open all night. In the morning, a fresh breeze pulled me out of a hard sleep. My body ached so much. What a rough night of tossing and turning.

I pushed my window wide open. An uproar of birdsong flooded in.

My mind yanked back to last night. The genocide content was scary. But connecting it to old people? Far-fetched.

I fumbled for my phone and texted Oma. *Read through those warning signs last night. I doubt it. Agree?*

Best to stay focused on perfecting my backhand and squeaking by in my classes.

After a stinging hot shower, I felt like myself again. I joined everyone in the kitchen. But a tug in my stomach reminded me about last night as I watched my family buzz about.

My dad looked up from his reading. "Oma said you were deep into homework, so we left you alone."

He waited for me to reply. All I could do was nod.

"What was the assignment?"

"World History. We're studying genocide." I wanted that to be enough. I knew it wouldn't be.

"Interesting!" he said with the type of enthusiasm I would save for winning the lottery. "You know, there's a good section in this book about the European wars. Do you need more information?"

He leafed through the book in his hands. Then he thrust it across the table so I was staring at another gritty black-and-white image of death and destruction.

"Just what I need to see over breakfast, Dad!" I cried, pushing the book back his way.

"Dad is fascinated by war and fighting, as long as it's history, not the latest video game," Wally grumbled.

I tried thinking of a way to give Wally a hard time. Then I felt that little tug again. Had all of those people in the genocide stories lived these boring little moments with their families? Before they were snatched away forever? I would be so glad when school was out for the summer.

"Fifteen minutes, Wally" was all I could come up with.

I looked forward to our morning walk. Today, I needed time to get my head together. I felt better than last night. But my worry about Oma wouldn't go away.

I dropped Wally off at his school and continued walking. When I reached the coffee shop, I squeezed into my usual spot between my friends. This was my chance to confirm my worry was ridiculous.

"Did you finish the history assignment?" I asked.

Jonah looked insulted.

"Did you?" Melissa asked.

"Almost. Disturbing, isn't it?" I tried.

"Definitely," Jonah said. Melissa nodded.

I sipped my drink, weighing whether to say more.

"Jonah," Melissa said, nudging him behind me. "Don't look now, but Alia is deep in thought."

"I know," Jonah whispered. A smile brightened his voice. "It's so unusual . . . I don't want to disturb her. You know, like waking up someone who's sleepwalking. She could hurt herself."

I was supposed to find it funny, but I felt annoyed. We had an unspoken rule that our teasing would not get mean. My next question about the homework stuck in my throat.

"Let's go," I said instead.

While we walked, Melissa entertained us with stories from the community theater musical she was helping put on. She worked with props, costumes, and makeup. She was a talented actress and singer, too, but she had trouble getting parts. Her sights were on breaking out of the small-town mold after high school.

When we reached the school, we peeled off to get ready for the day. We never said goodbye or planned our next meetup. Our lives were so intertwined, we didn't have to.

Passing under the school mascot banner, I left behind the bright morning light for the dim hallways. At least the organized chaos of school would help me leave last night's worries behind.

CHAPTER 6

As I entered World History later that morning, my mind was on my next tennis match. Winning this weekend meant advancing to regionals.

When I finally focused on the moment, it was too late to get my defenses up. Images bombarded me from the flat screen mounted on the wall. People fleeing war. People suffering in refugee camps. People crying for their loved ones. People lying dead in fields.

Every day, Mr. Carver wrote a quote on the whiteboard to get us thinking. Usually, the quotes didn't make much sense. I read today's a few times to make sure I understood: *Most events of genocide are marked by massive indifference, silence, and inactivity.*

The dread returned. My struggles weren't over with this subject.

Mr. Carver's no-nonsense voice called the class to

order. He switched off the slideshow. A document filled the screen.

"First, we explored different types of conflicts," Mr. Carver said. "Someone give us a refresher."

No surprise when Mary piped up. She was our class's bookworm. I took notes while she reviewed common reasons for conflict. Things like race and ethnic tension. Religion. Money. Not enough natural resources for everyone.

I thought back to the conversation with Oma. Maybe there was an answer in today's discussion.

"Good, good," Mr. Carver said. "The homework gave you examples of how some of these conflicts became genocides. Which one grabbed you in some way? What was most surprising?"

Andrew spoke up. "The one right here in our own country. Where they forced people to go through surgery so they couldn't have kids. It gave me nightmares. Selective breeding. It's sick and gross and disturbed."

Everyone nodded or shivered.

"Good example," Mr. Carver said. "What else?"

"I guess I was surprised at how many have happened," said Trudie. "I mean, we hear about the Holocaust. But all of the others I'd never heard about before—"

"Yeah," Frank interrupted. "Even in places I always thought were peaceful. Like Australia, with all its cute kangaroos and koala bears. Man, why can't people get along?"

The class started chiming in with "I know" and "Peace, baby" and other comments sprinkled with laughter. But it was an uncomfortable laughter about an uncomfortable subject.

"Does it matter if a conflict is officially declared a genocide?" Mr. Carver asked. "Isn't all oppression simply oppression? Should it be stopped no matter what?"

Jonah spoke up. "Well, if it's declared genocide, then the world has to try and stop it."

"So, if it isn't recognized as genocide, the world never gets involved?" Mr. Carver asked.

"Seems like there's always some peacekeeping mission

going on somewhere," said Peter. "And celebrities or politicians taking on causes, trying to protect some group of people. New dictators, new wars somewhere. They don't call all of those genocides."

"So maybe the world gets involved a lot," Mr. Carver said. "Is that good? Should the world always be getting in the middle of a particular country's business?"

"Yes! If we don't, all of these horrible things happen." I was surprised to hear the words escape my mouth. Mr. Carver was too.

"True, Alia." He raised his eyebrows. "A lot of horrible things have happened. And most of those did lead to some sort of action."

He ran his finger down a list. "There was public outcry. Diplomatic appeals. Sometimes financial pressure. Sometimes military action. And yet, we could ask whether these actions always helped. Or if they happened too slowly. Why would that be?"

He kept his eyes on me, expecting a second contribution for the day.

"Maybe they got involved too late because nobody could get a straight story about what was really happening," I suggested. My face flushed. "Or the leaders were so evil they didn't care what the rest of the world thought. I don't know. It just seems like a big mess."

"Ah, you make an interesting point," he said, clapping his hands once. Was he making fun of me? "How does a government or the world decide? Number one, is there oppression happening? Number two, does it mean others should push in and insist that it stop?"

"But right is right, and wrong is wrong." There I went again, blurting out a response and risking too much attention.

"It should be that easy, I agree." Mr. Carver gave me one of his rare smiles. "But we are studying example after example where it didn't seem to be. So, I want you all to have a chance to pretend you're in the driver's seat."

He scrolled to a new page describing a new assignment. The class groaned.

"Pick an example from all of our readings. Explain the evidence for genocide. Evaluate the actions that were taken." He gave us his *I-mean-business* look. "I'll know if you're copying ideas from experts. Consider this a reminder about plagiarism. Cite your sources. Explain why you agree with what was done or what you would have done differently. Any questions?"

"When is it due?" Jonah asked. Always the planner.

"I'm giving you three weeks," Mr. Carver said. "I want depth in these papers. This will be your last big assignment for the school year. You have the rest of the class to start thinking about what case study you're going to use. Grab me if you want to talk it through."

Kids started shifting in their seats. I glanced at Jonah and Melissa. They shot me amazed looks. I'd be hearing from them later about my speaking up in class.

I tried to pick a case study. But my brain wouldn't settle down. The conversation with Oma was all I could think about. Her reply to my morning text hadn't comforted me.

Maybe read the warning signs again, she'd written.

The rest of the day dragged miserably. Nothing eased my mind. Not even tennis practice. Everything irritated me.

Usually, the hollow *ping* of the ball ricocheting off rackets formed a comforting rhythm. It guided my back-and-forth dance over the red clay. Today, it gave me a headache.

Usually, sweat trickling down my back reassured me I was working hard. Today, it was an uncomfortable distraction, making me crankier by the minute.

And usually, I liked to join in on the light chitchat with my teammates, encouraging and congratulating one another on our moves. Today, I wanted people to shut up so I could think.

"What's up?" people kept asking me. But I just kept playing. How could I explain something I didn't know how to explain?

Coach Johnson reamed me out. Nothing too severe, but he was stressed about the upcoming match. I didn't try to defend myself while he went through my practice faults one by one. I apologized and promised to be back on target tomorrow.

My teammate Charlotte offered me a ride home. I accepted after texting Melissa not to wait for me. Charlotte was a good sport. She didn't gab at a hundred miles an hour or ask embarrassing questions.

"Bad day" was all I had to tell her. She patted my knee, turned up the tunes, and left me alone. It was so kind, I wanted to cry. Within a few minutes, she had me at my driveway. I smiled in thanks and grabbed my gear.

I didn't know what I was going to do about the World History assignment. I just knew home gave me the right vibes to sort it out.

CHAPTER 7

When I entered my house, Oma was sitting with Wally in the living room. They were looking at his word puzzles.

I glanced at his tablet and saw *Toe* _____. Wally was trying, and failing, to be patient with Oma. She liked to pretend to struggle with his quizzes.

"I think it's *Toe the line*," she said.

He rolled his eyes. "Obviously."

He increased the level and flashed a new puzzle.

Oma put her hand on my arm. "Help me with this one," she said.

nOeUcCkH!

I laughed because it fit the way Wally was behaving.

"*Pain in the neck*," I answered.

Oma and Wally looked at me, surprised. Their shock irritated me.

"I'm not stupid." I headed to my room.

In the hall, I overheard my dad speaking. The mention of Oma made me pause. I looked into my parents' room. Dad was video chatting with someone.

"I don't know how she can fight this," Dad said. "But I think she should try."

"Well, there's the lawsuit being organized," the man on the other end said. "But CLEAR is making it hard on those who join it. She could end up in worse shape. You heard about the incident in Florida, right?"

Dad nodded and rubbed his eyes. "This is bananas. She's practically healthier than the rest of the family!"

"My mother too," the man said. "Let me do some more research and call you back."

Dad disconnected and stared at his bed. I stared at his back. I was afraid to ask about what I'd just heard.

"Dinner!" Mom cried from the kitchen.

A startled sound escaped me. Dad noticed me in the doorway. He looked very tired, like he'd been carrying this worry for too long. His parents died many years ago. Mom said Oma had always treated him like a son.

"Let's eat, Zippy," he said. I'd earned the nickname when I was tiny and ran around so fast that he and Mom couldn't catch me. It comforted me to hear it.

As we sat down for dinner, Oma touched my shoulder. Her look said she was sorry. I flashed her a goofy face so she'd know it was okay.

We ate in silence. I noticed Dad giving Mom a glance that meant something was up.

"So." Mom turned to Oma. "What did your results say?"

Oma looked up. "Exactly what I expected. I'm fine."

"And?" Mom prodded.

"And what?"

"What's your SSS?"

Oma looked amused. "I don't agree with the idea. I'm not acknowledging it exists."

"What's an SSS?" I asked.

Everyone swiveled toward me. They were surprised to hear me join the discussion.

"It means Senior Situation Score," Dad said. "The government is using these scores to make care plans for senior citizens. And to assign them housing. The higher your score, the better your chances for staying independent longer."

I suddenly felt very queasy. "Does your score mean they want you to move?" I asked Oma. She currently lived in her own home.

"They can say what they want," she answered. "But I plan to stay."

None of this was what my mom wanted to hear. "I just want you to get the best care when you're ready for it."

Oma shook her head. "I'm not ready for it."

"Then move in here," Dad said. "That will buy some time. I'm making calls, seeing what options there are."

"Tim, you're going to make it worse," my mom fretted. "They'll cut off her funds. Then what?"

Oma was still smiling, but there was an edge to it now. "Thank you, Tim. I know you mean well. But I didn't live this long to give in to a new whim sweeping this country like a bad virus. Ava, honey, I know you mean well too. But trust your *mutter*. I will fight it."

I remembered something I overheard on my dad's video call. "What's this group called CLEAR?" I asked. I wondered if they were something else Oma would need to fight.

"I'm glad to see you paying attention," Oma said.

"What are they trying to do?" I asked. "What exactly is happening?"

"The group stands for Citizens for Logical and Effective Application of Resources." Dad spoke in a disgusted tone. "CLEAR pushed for the new rules requiring senior citizens to take medical tests and move into comfort care centers."

I picked at my food, thinking hard.

"What would happen to your house?" I asked Oma.

"I'd have to sell it. The money would go to the care center. Supposedly, it would be used to take care of me."

My mom started dishing out more food on our plates even though we didn't ask for it.

"The law is meant to help," she said. "What's good about people getting sick or hurt and dying in their own home, sometimes all alone? Or moving in with family who can't really cope?"

"What's good about our freedoms and choices being taken away?" Oma asked, her usually calm voice sounding sharp. "Is this the prize for reaching a seasoned age? Losing your civil rights?"

"It's meant to show respect and care," my mom said. Her face turned red, and her eyes got watery. "We're making sure seniors are protected. You know, there are unethical people trying to take their money or promising them outrageous ways of living longer. They can be taken advantage of."

Dad shook his head. "Things are going too far. And now CLEAR is getting people even more worked up. It's turning nasty."

"What if someone refuses to move?" I tried to keep my voice steady.

Dad shrugged. "Nobody is sure. The government is threatening action, but it's untested right now."

"Untested *here*. But in Florida . . ." My mom didn't continue.

"What?" I insisted.

Oma fixed me with her gaze. "They took the homes of people who refused to move and forced them into a center. And when some of the families tried to stop it, they were arrested."

Everyone was quiet again.

I couldn't sit any longer. I pulled back from the table. Most of the food on my plate was untouched.

"I'm going to eat this later," I said. "Practice took it out of me today. I'll be in my room."

"How is that assignment coming, Alia?" Oma asked.

I knew what she was really asking. And I knew how to answer.

"I have a lot of research to do. But I think I'm on the right track. I'll keep you posted."

46

CHAPTER 8

My whole body tingled with worry when I got to my room. The genocide readings from Mr. Carver were already too hard for me. Now I wanted to create a whole new case study instead of using an example he'd given us? I didn't even know if I'd find enough details for my paper.

Where to even start?

It was time for yoga so I could get in the right headspace for this. My mind went on autopilot as I stretched and slowed my breathing.

Then I reread the assignment. After three times, I still felt lost. This was exactly why my parents had found me a tutor. The woman was nice during our weekly sessions, but she told my parents everything we did. I wasn't ready for them to know about this. Still, she could help me with Mr. Carver's materials.

Jonah would help if I asked. But his teasing earlier still

stung. And Melissa probably needed a tutor as badly as I did. Mr. Carver came to mind. Would he laugh me out of the school or help me? Too risky to find out.

I had to help Oma, but I was in over my head. Why didn't I know more smart people who liked this kind of stuff?

Maybe I could trick Wally into doing my homework. Could I figure out a way to get his help without him knowing? I could at least pick up some tips on how he studied.

After yoga, I headed straight to Wally's room before I could lose my nerve. I knocked three times.

"What?" he asked through the door.

"It's me. Open up. I need to ask you something."

After an eternity, he opened the door a crack. "Am I in trouble?"

Interesting, I thought. Normally I would have explored this to use later. Right now, I had a mission.

"Not my issue to worry about," I said. "I need to interview you for a school assignment."

He opened the door all the way. "*You* interview *me*? Why? What's the homework?" He was suspicious, and I didn't blame him.

I plunged in, using words teachers and parents tossed about. I said it was for a project to see if middle graders were really ready for high school. It took a few minutes, but I convinced him to show me how he did his homework.

Back in my room later, my brain didn't know what to do with how I felt. I had some good ideas about how to tackle my project. But I kind of hated Wally. Or at least resented him. Why was it so easy for him and hard for me? Where was the fairness in that?

I found an unopened pack of index cards Mom bought me months ago. First, I would try Wally's way of organizing information.

I brainstormed different words I'd heard used to describe old people. Then I made category cards for *laws*, *problems*, and *money*.

Next, I searched online, trying different combinations of my words. Page after page of results came up.

My stomach knotted. *Keep going*, I told myself.

I scanned through the top articles. I'd been surprised to learn Wally didn't actually read all of the information in an article. Instead, he found the main point in the first few paragraphs. Then he scanned subsections and any graphics. He would even skip to the final paragraphs.

It pissed me off that my tutor never taught me that strategy. I was going to try it with this project.

But even using Wally's strategy, my research went slowly. I passed over impossible sentences. I created a growing list of vocabulary words to look up later. Still, I found some important details to write on the index cards.

The facts started stacking up.

The Senior Situation Score was based on several things. Age, of course. But also how healthy a person was. How much family help they had. How much money they had saved. How sharp their thinking was. Even their attitude. A person's SSS determined their care plan and housing.

I needed to ask Oma about her score.

The "aging problem" came up a lot in my research.

This argument said there were way more old people than young people in the country. Not enough caregivers. Not enough money. Not enough time to figure out a solution. That reminded me of the reasons for conflict we talked about in Mr. Carver's class.

I found an upsetting story about a court battle involving a hospital in another part of the country. The hospital had put really sick elderly patients in one space. Workers wouldn't give them treatment so they would die sooner.

Another story was even harder to read. A bunch of teens—kids my age—ganged up on an old man. Their teasing got out of control. They hurt him, and he died later. The kids weren't punished because the police said his SSS suggested he was going to die soon anyway.

I had no idea this stuff was going on. Were bad things like this happening here too?

"Bedtime." The voice of my clock startled me. Yikes. I'd been at it for three hours. Definitely a first. I looked at my work spread across my floor. My thoughts ping-ponged back and forth.

I needed to submit this as my final assignment. But could I afford to roll the dice on my grade? I had to play this game right to not mess up my future. There was still time to pick something from Mr. Carver's list. But I'd pretty much told Oma I would do this. And I couldn't calm my growing fear about what was going on.

I'd decide for sure in the morning. Maybe I could talk it through with Oma. Or I could take a risk and ask Mr. Carver.

I remembered him mentioning the word *firebreak* in class. Somehow, it seemed important. I typed it into the dictionary.

A barrier of cleared or plowed land intended to stop the spread of a forest or grass fire.

Not it. I fished through my class notes until I found it: *A measure taken to arrest the advance of anything dangerous or harmful. Barriers to prevent the spread of conflict.*

Prevent the spread of conflict.

Fat chance that my little paper could create a firebreak. But I went to sleep with the word floating into my dreams.

CHAPTER 9

The next morning, I stumbled into the kitchen for breakfast. My eyes felt like big swollen blobs, and my head throbbed. Sleep had outrun me last night.

Everyone seemed to be in their own world this morning. Dad and Wally were reading their books. Mom was eating in between getting other things done. Good. I was on edge. I didn't want to talk.

Unfortunately, Mom perked up when I passed her.

"You were up late," she said.

"Homework." I tossed fruit and protein powder into the blender.

Mom hovered nearby. She was pretending to wipe down the counter. But the counter was already spotless. She clearly had something to say.

"What's up?" I asked.

She set down her dishrag. "I just don't want you

worrying about the stuff we talked about last night. It's going to be okay. Oma will be fine."

Dad looked up but stayed quiet.

"I hope so," I said. "But it seems like there's a lot to worry about."

"People are spinning things the wrong way." Mom glanced at Dad, who wore a poker face. "Just stay focused on school. We'll work this out with Oma."

Her words crashed down and broke my last nerve.

"Stop treating me like I'm five," I snapped. "I need to know what's going on. Why aren't you more worried about her?"

Mom took a deep breath. "I am worried. That's why I want her to get things set up now before she gets older. Just let the grown-ups handle it."

I slammed my empty cup in the sink harder than I'd meant. But at least the BANG made my point.

"Doesn't seem like the grown-ups are doing a good job of handling this," I barked on my way out.

After dropping Wally off at his school, I took a detour.

Instead of heading to the coffee shop, I veered in a different direction. Soon I was in front of an apartment building painted peach with lime green trim. It looked cheery and normal. Flowery letters spelled out *Home Care Center* on a sign over the front entrance.

I walked the pathway around to the back. Several seniors were having coffee or tea on a terraced patio surrounded by a garden. A few looked up and smiled at me. The scents of jasmine and strong java reached my nose.

"Who do you want to see?" asked a woman in a sky-blue track suit. "I can tell you if they're up already."

Heat crept across my neck and face. I was prying where I didn't belong.

"No one. I was just checking the place out. It looks so pretty," I fumbled.

The woman smiled in a way that didn't actually seem happy. "Grandma or grandpa set to move?" she asked.

Tears came before I could get myself under control. I was in over my head. But I needed to know.

"Can I ask . . . did you want to move here?" I whispered.

The woman looked at me steadily. "No. It's possible I would have chosen to come to a place like this in a few years. But moving here now . . . it wasn't my choice. But what's done is done, and I'm trying to make the best of it. This place isn't horrible. I've heard of worse. I just miss my old community."

My "thanks" came out in another whisper. I hurried on to school.

I tried my best to ask questions and make comments. But I couldn't focus. I gave Jonah and Melissa a vague excuse about why I'd missed our morning meetup. A quick nap over lunch got me through the afternoon.

By practice time, I had my nerves under control. I needed to stay in the zone to be ready for tournament rounds. Today went better. Coach even gave me a thumbs-up as we packed up.

"Want a ride?" Charlotte asked as we headed into the parking lot.

"Actually, that would be amazing. I'm toast."

For a few blocks, we chilled to music. Then:

"I'm starved," she said. "Can you grab the trail mix in my bag for me? I'll share."

I twisted around to the back seat and fished in her gear bag. There was the snack—right next to a CLEAR brochure.

My heart stopped. Why would she have that? Maybe I wasn't the only one worrying after all.

"You know about CLEAR?" I blurted out.

Charlotte gave me a puzzled look. "Of course. Why?"

"I just heard about them. Thought I was alone in this, I guess."

That made her laugh. "No way. Do you want to come to a meeting with me?"

I froze. "Wait. Why would I go to a meeting for CLEAR?"

"Because it's the best way to get involved so we can take care of the problem," she said. "My parents are super involved."

My heart fell into my stomach. I couldn't believe what I was hearing. "What exactly is the problem?"

Charlotte turned onto my street. "I mean, we all get

older, right? But the aging population is a total mess. The system can't handle this many old people. Something's got to be done."

"But we're talking about people like my grandma." My voice broke. Fear flooded back into my body.

She pulled up in front of my home. "I know. You're not the only one with grandparents. But there aren't enough resources for younger generations. You can read more about it in the brochure. Take it and let me know if you want to come to a meeting."

I shoved the brochure back into her bag and got out of the car without a word. Charlotte shrugged and sped away.

Somehow, I figured kids my age would not be okay with this stuff. Charlotte blew that idea out of the water.

Everything from this day reinforced my decision about Mr. Carver's assignment. Making the case that there were warning signs of an elderly genocide wouldn't be easy. But I had to do this. For Oma. For me.

I wouldn't share details with my family, or even Jonah and Melissa. Handling their reactions could wait.

CHAPTER 10

Over the next three weeks, I did it. I lied to my friends, saying my project would focus on what happened in Cambodia in the 1970s. I avoided Jonah's offers to help me with the assignment. And I turned in my paper with my wild theory about a looming elderly genocide.

I wanted to retrieve the file the second it landed in Mr. Carver's server. But once you put a file in his folder, you couldn't take it out.

I was finished. I'd probably fail. The school would take away my sports for senior year. And where would I be without them? Not being able to play would throw my whole future in the air. But my mind turned back to Oma and other senior citizens. I hoped Mr. Carver would understand why I'd taken this risk.

I made a last-second decision to walk over to Oma's place. It was time to share what I'd done. She'd probably figured it out already since she'd planted the idea in the first place. But letting her in on the secret could help me survive the wait for Mr. Carver's reaction.

When I got to Oma's street, I stopped cold. There was a moving van in front of her house. A government car next to it had the words *Transition Agency* on its side. Oma's front door was open. Voices spilled out into the front yard.

I sprinted inside in a panic.

Oma stood in the middle of the living room, surrounded by boxes. Two grim-faced men were supervising her packing.

My sudden appearance caught them all off guard. The two men looked mad. Oma looked alarmed.

"Oma? What's going on?" I asked.

"No family allowed!" one of the men barked at me.

"Leave her alone," Oma said. "She didn't know."

She picked her way through the mess and pulled me into a hug.

"It's not my choice to move, but making a scene won't help," she whispered in my ear. "Stay strong with me, okay?"

I couldn't hold back my tears. "Why is this happening? Where are you going? We need to call Mom and Dad. Maybe they can stop it."

Oma hugged me tighter. "I'm moving to one of the nearby care center apartments. And your parents know already. We were going to tell you later."

That stunned me into silence. They'd kept this from me.

Oma walked me outside. "I'll call once I'm settled," she said. "I promise."

She gently pushed me into motion. When I turned the corner, I broke into a run for home. Anger and fear pumped me full of adrenaline. Nothing about this was right. How could the government just force someone to give up their home for no good reason? Why weren't more people doing something to stop this? And why did my parents keep this from me?

I ran up to the house and found Mom pulling weeds in the garden.

"How could you not tell me?" I screeched.

"Whoa. What? Tell you what?" she asked.

"About Oma moving." My tears came back.

"Oh honey. I'm sorry," she said. "We were going to tell you tonight. Wait. How did you find out?"

"I was just there. Two awful men are making her pack. Why aren't you trying to stop them?"

She tried to hug me, but I shook her off.

"We can't," she said, her voice shaking. "Families are getting arrested if they try to intervene. We can't risk that. I know this is a shock. But I promise she's going to be okay."

"I don't believe you!" I yelled. "You're probably happy about it."

I pushed past her and ran inside to my room.

The World History assignment popped into my head. I hadn't been able to tell Oma about it. But I knew now more than ever that something bad was going on. Even if Mr. Carver flunked me, I couldn't stay quiet.

CHAPTER 11

For the next few days, I tried to stay focused on school and on tennis. Keeping my head in the game was hard. But her move didn't stop Oma from showing up as always. That comforted me. I won two tough matches and advanced in the tournament.

Then, it was time to face the music. Mr. Carver spent class talking about how we'd done on the assignment. He sent out our graded files a few minutes before the bell. I planned to wait for some privacy to look at mine.

"Alia," Mr. Carver called. "Can you stay for a short chat? I'll give you an excused tardy."

It didn't seem like I could say no. I avoided stares from Jonah and Melissa, who hovered nearby until Mr. Carver shooed them away. Waves of hallway noise filled the room before the door closed behind them.

I expected a lecture. But at least I'd tried this time.

I'd really tried. I hoped that counted, especially since Mr. Carver knew how hard school was for me. He had to follow my IEP.

"Your paper was really well done," he said.

I waited, sure I'd heard wrong.

"Alia? Do you understand?"

"No." Best to be honest at this point.

He sat down at a desk near me. "Your paper surprised me."

"Really?" I didn't know how to feel. It was my dream and my fear all rolled into one.

"I don't mean that in an insulting way. But since you tend to struggle, it seemed good for us to talk about this project. I kept expecting you to come to me for help, but you didn't."

I got it now. He thought I'd cheated.

"Mr. Carver, I'm an honest person and I would never cheat. I did the work myself."

He threw up his hands and laughed. "Okay, okay. I'll admit it did cross my mind. But only for a few seconds.

Even though it isn't your normal work, I can tell it's your effort."

"How?"

"Because it has *Alia* all over it in terms of how it's written," he said, smiling. "But you are making progress in how you put together your thoughts. That's what's important."

He opened my file on his tablet and scrolled through it.

"The organization and intensity in this paper . . . it's good work. In fact—" His smile disappeared. "Your theory deserves attention. I'd like to offer you a chance at extra credit. Research this more and submit a second paper. It will help raise your grade. And it will give you another reason to keep going with your investigation."

"Investigation?" I could barely keep up with this conversation.

"What's going on with the elderly is concerning," he said. "I don't know if it's racing toward genocide. That will feel like a huge stretch to a lot of people. But you pointed out real-life examples that fit the warning signs. This type of information could help people take a pause. I assume you thought of this because of Ellen."

I forgot he knew my grandma. She had been friends with his parents for a long time. Tears formed in my eyes. I desperately wanted to not cry in front of him.

The warning bell rang for the next class.

"My grandma saw my genocide homework and said some stuff that got me thinking. She had to take a bunch of medical tests. Then she was forced to move. It's scaring me."

Mr. Carver nodded. "Then do this project. Focus even more on what firebreak strategies might be used."

I hesitated. Doing this paper alone almost killed me.

"You could finish over the summer and submit it when we start back up. I can still adjust your grade for your senior transcript," he added. "This helps with your academic probation problem, doesn't it? It shows you're making a serious effort. And you'll be helping Ellen. I know you're stressing about all of this. Will you at least think about it?"

I nodded. The panic came back. I felt such relief about

not failing the paper. But zero relief when it came to my worry about senior citizens.

"I will write you up a new assignment sheet," Mr. Carver said. "That will give you some structure to work with."

We walked out of the classroom and parted without another word.

I texted Oma to arrange a meetup at the coffee shop after school.

Her wise words could steer me on what to do.

CHAPTER 12

I found Oma tucked away in the back of the café. Her large mug of black coffee was half-finished.

"I know you don't have a lot of time. Did you eat already?" Oma reached over and squeezed my hand. Her hair was up in an elegant bun. She looked like she'd walked off the page of a fashion magazine for mature women. But her exercise clothes meant she'd just taken her daily three-mile walk.

I squeezed her hand back. "I'm good. Nibbling on and off all day. Don't want anything heavy before my match tonight."

"Okay, then why the urgent need to meet?" she asked. "Not that I don't want to see you any chance I can."

"Remember my World History assignment about genocide?" I asked.

"Of course," she said. "We had a good conversation about that."

Here it went. I took a deep breath and then rushed through it.

"Well, I focused on what's happening to senior citizens now. And I asked whether there could be a new genocide in the works. I expected Mr. Carver to flunk me and laugh me out of the school. But he didn't. He gave me a good grade. And he wants me to do another project on it. He thinks I'm onto something."

I shouldn't have been nervous about Oma's reaction. She grabbed me in a hug and kissed my cheek.

"You smart girl," she muttered. "I hoped you were putting two and two together. And how brave to tackle that as your example. Will you do this extra project?"

I shrugged. "I was going to ask you about it. I'm worried about what's going on. But it's too much to do anything on my own."

Oma fished in her backpack and brought out a small

notebook. She scribbled some information on a page. Then she ripped it out to give to me.

She'd written *Generativity* and a contact number.

"They will help you," she said, leaning in closer to be heard.

"Who are they?" I asked.

"They're a group putting together a campaign to challenge what's going on. You'll be surprised at some of the people involved."

My next question was easy to guess.

"Yes, I'm involved," said Oma. "But we really need the involvement of young people. You can add a level of attention that elderly folks won't get on our own."

I shook my head, and she smiled.

"I am so proud of you. None of us can do this alone. It's about working together." She sipped her coffee, looking deep in thought. "It would be even more powerful if you could recruit some of your friends. The more young voices, the better."

I laughed at that. "I'm not exactly your most convincing spokesperson."

"You're selling yourself short, Alia. Talk to Jonah and Melissa first. They're your best friends. They'll have your back." Oma finished her coffee and started cleaning up the table to leave.

I remembered something I needed to ask her. "Oma? Can you tell me what your SSS is? Please?"

She studied me, deciding what to say. "It's high. Don't worry about me for now. My health is good. My brain is functioning well. My score won't start dropping anytime soon."

"What will happen when it drops?" I pressed. "What will they do?"

"They'll start taking away more of my freedoms," Oma said. "It will either be several restrictions all at once, or a slow drip of things I'm no longer allowed to do on my own."

I pushed further. "I read that how much you cooperate can affect your score. If they find out you're involved in some kind of protest movement, won't that drop your score?"

"Good for you," Oma said, smiling. "I'm glad you're digging. I don't know, but I can't sit by and do nothing. I'm willing to take the risk. Remember what you're learning in class. We all have to decide for ourselves. Will we stand by and watch as something happens that we know is wrong? I've decided for myself. Now you need to decide for you."

We left the coffee shop and hugged outside.

Her parting words stayed with me the rest of the afternoon: "Welcome to the cause, Alia. It's been waiting for you."

CHAPTER 13

I stretched my calves while waiting for Jonah and Melissa to connect. I'd aced my tennis match. But my muscles were angry, and I was drained.

Jonah appeared online first. "I saw the end of your game. A little aggressive today, weren't we?"

"Guaranteeing my ranking. I need it high for the scouts." I gently bent over toward my knees until I was at the point of discomfort.

Melissa popped on, and Jonah jumped right in. "So, tennis star, we're dying to know why Mr. Carver held you back. Whatever happened, we'll help you anyway we can. You know that."

Melissa added, "Remember. Teachers have to be harsh. Don't worry too much about your grade. I'm sure he'll let you do some extra credit."

Once again, people assumed I'd screwed up. Still, telling

them the truth had me nervous. I tried to snap out of it. These were my best friends forever. I trusted them with so much. Time to trust them with this.

"I'm going to send you my paper. He actually liked it. A lot."

"What?!" they cried.

"I'll try to not be completely insulted," I said.

"Sorry," Jonah said. "But tell us more."

Melissa nodded.

"He thinks there could be some truth to what I wrote. He offered me extra credit to keep going with the work," I said.

"What?!" they both cried again.

My anger boiled up. "Yes, I understand it's a huge shocker that I'm doing something right in class."

Jonah and Melissa winced.

"But he thinks I'm onto something," I finished.

"What does that mean?" Melissa asked. "Didn't you write about Cambodia?"

I took a huge breath and jumped in with the truth. That

I had lied. That I'd written about a potential new genocide in the making.

When I was done, my friends were too stunned to speak. After a long pause, Melissa shook her head.

"Wait," she said. "Old people are going to be killed off? *That's* what you wrote about?"

"I just looked at what's going on using the early warning signs," I explained.

Jonah's voice, usually calm, sounded like Melissa doing fake shrill opera. *"And he liked that? And thinks it could be true?"*

Stinging tears pushed to the fronts of my eyes. I took three deep breaths.

"We're trying to hear you out, honey," Melissa said.

"Then help me by reading my paper and the new assignment sheet. Give me some ideas for the project. And don't write me off as totally stupid," I added. "It really hurts."

They stared at me for an eternity.

"Sorry," Jonah said quietly.

"Me too," Melissa added.

We disconnected without saying goodbye. I sent my documents to them. I didn't have high hopes. Maybe they couldn't relate. Melissa's grandparents were gone already. Jonah still had two grandparents alive. But his community seemed to help their elderly more. And I think they had their own rules and laws, so maybe this didn't affect them. I'd have to ask Jonah about that.

How would I bring this up with Mom and Dad? They seemed so tired and distracted in the evenings now. Sometime at breakfast would be better.

My chance came faster than I expected.

The next morning, Dad sat next to Wally at the table. He had a worn book propped against his coffee cup. He read from it and jotted in a notebook.

"Your assignment on genocide got me interested in reading up on the subject," he said. "How did you do on that homework?"

"Well, I got an extra credit assignment from it," I said as I moved to the fridge.

Mom and Dad did the silent parent thing with their eyes. Then Dad said, "I wish you would have asked us for more help."

I tossed a frozen banana in the blender and sighed. They once again assumed I'd crashed and burned.

"Actually, Mr. Carver really liked my paper. The extra credit is because he wants me to take my research further."

I waited for "That's great, honey!" and "Way to go!" Instead, I got stunned silence. I shot them both a glare.

Dad recovered first. "Wow. That's a very pleasant surprise. Very pleasant. Sorry. Tell us more."

Mom chimed in. "Excellent news. Yes. Let's hear more."

I loudly blended my frozen fruit to delay my answer. Then I said, "I'd like to give you my paper to read. But you need to keep an open mind."

"Okay," Dad said. "Why, exactly?"

"Because I took a risk on the genocide theme. I couldn't ignore the signs."

"What signs?" Mom asked.

I sat at the table. Wally didn't even look up at me.

"All of the stuff going on with elderly citizens. I used that as the focus."

"You what?!" Mom asked.

"Um, Alia. That sounds like a stretch," Dad said.

"Are you suggesting there's a genocide happening? Just because things are being done to make sure seniors have the care they need?" Mom asked. "My mom got you on this, didn't she?"

"Mr. Carver agrees," I told her.

"Mr. Carver is probably excited you took homework seriously for once," she shot back.

"Whoa, you two," Dad said.

I tried keeping my temper in check. "At least read my paper. Look at the early warning signs. We should be doing something about it."

Mom waved her hands around. "We *are* doing something. We're making sure seniors are protected."

"By taking away their freedoms?" I looked at Dad. "Do you agree with what's happening?"

I knew he didn't. But would he back me up here?

He took a long sip of his coffee. "I agree with you both. Genocide is a serious accusation here. But the laws and new proposals need to be challenged."

"Did you know Charlotte and her family are involved in CLEAR?" I asked. "They seem so nice and reasonable. How could they buy into this stuff?"

Dad just shook his head.

Mom slapped her hands on the table. "I forbid you from getting more involved in this, Alia. Stay focused on doing well with school and tennis. Don't get caught up in the drama some people are trying to make."

They were always telling me to step up my game with my studies. Well, I did. And it had been really hard. Now they were disappointed. No way to win with this one.

"Read it or don't read it, whatever." I gulped down the rest of my breakfast, then left.

I waited for Wally out front. When he joined me, we began walking. After a few steps, he said, "I'll help you."

I was so lost in my own thoughts that I didn't follow. "Help me with what?" I looked him over. I had to smile at the sight of his droopy basketball shorts hanging down to his skinny knees.

"Help you with your extra credit assignment," he said.

"Wait, what? Why? Everyone else seems to think I'm wrong."

Wally shrugged. "Not everyone. Your teacher. Oma. And others. Can I read your paper?"

No way I wanted my genius little brother reading my homework.

"Maybe," I said. "I don't see how you can help me. Still, your show of support is a nice change."

We reached Wally's school, and he headed up the front steps. At the door, he called back, "I *am* known for my research skills. Let me help." Then he disappeared inside.

Go figure. My little brother was the one who had my back.

CHAPTER 14

The cold metal chair chilled me to the bone through my running shorts. Oma showed no signs of being uncomfortable. Her calm kept me calm. Otherwise, I would have slipped out already. Coming to this meeting had been a mistake.

Ann, the Generativity leader, kept glancing my way and smiling. Oma had introduced us when we'd first arrived. Ann had gently squeezed my arm in welcome. Having someone my age join their meetings was a big deal.

More chairs in the small room filled up. Randomly, someone would reach over and squeeze my arm with a smile. This usually prompted Oma to give me her own affectionate squeeze. I felt like a piece of fruit being tested for ripeness.

"Let's get started," Ann finally called out. "First,

introductions. Can new attendees please stand and share a little about yourselves?"

All eyes immediately landed on me. Oma put her hand under my elbow and nudged me up. My mouth turned to cotton. My chest tightened until breathing seemed impossible.

Ann moved closer and smiled wide. "This is Ellen's granddaughter, Alia."

I could only nod.

"Alia has a school project that fits well with our work. We are very glad to help her. And we hope she'll be able to help us," Ann continued. "Anything to add, Alia?"

I tried desperately to talk but only managed a smile. I hoped they wouldn't all rush up to squeeze me to death. Oma tugged me back down into my seat.

Two grown-ups introduced themselves. Then Ann pointed to a small sign taped to the wall near the front. It had *Generativity* written in simple letters.

"An explanation for those who are new and a refresher for those who are not," she said. "Our group's name comes from the idea that aging generations want to guide younger generations by passing along knowledge."

Ann next waved up a man named Matthew to give an activity report.

Matthew read from his notes. "Laws around managing the population are coming this fall. There's the proposal to move seniors into specific zones. That's the biggest thing we're gearing up to fight."

This comment triggered lots of frustrated mumbling.

Matthew kept going. "And there have been more reports of violence. I'm sure you've seen some of these on the news. We have our monitoring systems in place now. We know there are more incidents than what are being reported."

His words brought a heavy silence to the room. Oma squeezed my hand. Then she moved to the front of the room to give her own report. I suddenly realized how involved she was.

"We're almost ready to hit hard on our Generativity messages," she shared. "We need to present the facts in a way that clicks for people. And I think the voices of young people can have an impact. I haven't heard of any other groups with a youth movement in the works. We could be the first and inspire others."

Oma returned to her seat. Other people went to the front of the room to give updates. Everyone seemed to have their own assignment. But they also seemed to receive lots of support. Even though the thought scared me to death, maybe getting involved in Generativity was the best way to tackle my project. I couldn't handle doing it alone again.

After the big meeting ended, people shifted chairs around to work in smaller groups. Oma and I helped Ann open up snacks. I filled a paper cup with apple juice.

"What do you think, Alia?" Ann asked. "Do you want to organize a youth campaign?"

I felt way in over my head. "Can't I just do something behind the scenes?"

"We could find something, of course. All help is welcomed," Ann said. "But we're at a key point in putting together an information campaign for the summer. Would that fit with your school project?"

She must have seen my dread because she patted my shoulder.

"I know this may feel overwhelming at first. But I think there's someone who can help you get up to speed. He's a student from here but in the city right now doing an internship. He's very smart, very nice." Ann smiled at Oma. "All of us are willing to help out. But you might prefer to study with another young person."

She fished in her wallet and handed me a business card.

Eric Williams. Humanitarian in Training.

"Will you call Eric and think about it?" Ann asked. "If you do decide to do it, it would be great if you could come to the next meeting to share some ideas."

"Okay," I said. At least my voice worked this time.

Ann gestured for me to follow her. "Meanwhile, we should talk to Matthew. He's filled with ideas that will jumpstart your thinking."

I wanted to sprint out the door and forget about this whole business. But I couldn't abandon Oma.

By the time we left, I had a folder stuffed with printouts of news articles and other research Generativity members had collected. Two things filled me with dread.

First, my assignment had merely scratched the surface of what was happening.

Second, Generativity expected a lot from anyone getting involved in their campaign. The situation was turning urgent. They needed "all hands on deck," as the members said over and over.

I wanted to be a deckhand. But they wanted me to be the captain of my own little ship, and to fill it with other kids who wanted to be part of this adventure. I didn't know how to make that happen.

CHAPTER 15

Since learning about her involvement in CLEAR, I'd tried to ignore Charlotte during practice. But this was often impossible.

"You should come check it out," I heard her say. I was nearby, switching courts.

I glanced over. She'd pinned a CLEAR logo to the outside of her gear bag and was putting a stack of brochures on the bench. A few of our teammates were taking a look.

"Things are getting really bad," she went on. Loudly, so that I could hear. "I mean, do you want things like college aid money disappearing before you can use it? That's going to happen if we don't do something now."

Our coach butted in before she could say more. "Not the place, Charlotte. Put it all away and don't do it again." He gave everyone a stern look. "Stay focused on tennis when you're on these courts."

I was glad the coach had spoken up. But Charlotte's smirk made it hard to focus the rest of practice.

That night, Oma popped by to check on me. The untouched pile of research from the Generativity meeting sat stacked on my chair. She looked over my shoulder at what I was trying to read on my bed.

"Finals prep," I explained.

"Got it. I won't stay long." She moved to the chair and flipped open the folder. "How about I help you organize these notes this weekend?"

"It's okay. I'll get to it."

She leafed through the papers. "I'm happy to help."

Anger rushed through me. "Leave it. I said I'll do it."

Oma put the papers aside. "When?"

"When I'm *ready*." I hated being angry at my grandma. But I hated feeling pressured to do something I was unsure about. I had been trying to get okay with the idea that I could handle this. Why did she have to barge in and ruin it?

The long silence felt crushing.

"Do you not want to do this?" Oma finally asked. "Tell

me the truth. It's okay if you want to stop. I know we're asking a lot from you."

I suddenly couldn't see through my tears. She wrapped her arms around me. After a while, I found my voice.

"I want to do it and I don't want to do it. I know I'm stalling. Does that make sense?"

She hugged me tight. "It makes perfect sense. And I shouldn't be pushing you. It's something you have to figure out. Remember that you have lots of people who can help. But you ask for help if and when you're ready. Okay?"

I squeezed her back. "Okay," I whispered.

"What else is going on?" Oma asked. "Sounds like you're giving your mom the cold shoulder."

I should have known Oma would fish on this front. Mom must have bent her ear. "She's against all of this. Thinks things are just fine. Why is she not protecting you?"

Oma pulled away. "She thinks she *is* protecting me." She put up a hand to stop me from objecting. "I don't agree with her, of course. But not talking to her only deepens the divide. That isn't good in many ways."

When I didn't say anything, she nudged my foot. "Please keep that in mind."

"Got it," was all I could manage. I didn't like being mad at Mom. But she needed to get out of denial.

Oma stood and moved toward the door.

"Wait!" This was my chance to dig deeper about what I heard at the Generativity meeting. "I can't stand the thought of you being sent off somewhere else. That's what they mean by geographic zones, right?"

"Yes," Oma said. "That's why we have to come out in full force about all of this. We need to create doubt in people's minds. These proposals could be shoved through before anyone understands what they mean." She hugged me tight, then quietly disappeared.

I stared at the folder on my chair. Delaying wasn't an option anymore. Not if Oma could be sent away. I started scanning the papers. A lot of it was mountains above my reading level.

The business card for the intern guy fell out. Contacting him would be a big step. But I needed a thinking partner.

Wally was a possibility, but my mind kept coming back to Jonah. He seemed right for this.

I sent Jonah a text. Soon, his head filled the screen of my phone. "Hey there. What's up?"

I showed Jonah the pile of papers. "I'm playing the we've-been-friends-since-we-were-tiny card. I really, really, really need you to help me think through this extra credit project. Oma got me connected with an activist group. They asked me to organize a youth information campaign. I'm in way over my head."

Jonah studied me. "I read your report. It was good. I agree with Mr. Carver that you're onto something. But you don't have to do this."

"How can I not do this? But I'm scared out of my mind. I need my smart best friend who knows how to step up as a leader. Help me step up. Please." I stared him in the eye. I knew how to take charge on the tennis court. Maybe this wasn't any different.

Jonah stared back. At first, he had the hard-set look he got when he wasn't planning to budge. Then his look softened. The beginnings of a smile crept to the corners of his mouth. "Okay."

"Yes!" I moved in to kiss the screen.

"Enough, germ baby." He wiped the "contaminants" off his side of the screen. "If you're this determined, clearly it's important. Dare I ask if this could be a new Alia emerging?"

"Maybe. Or maybe this Alia has always been there, and you were unwilling to see her."

"Point made. Okay, I have to go. Let's talk tomorrow. Sleep well, my friend. And stop worrying so much." He started to sign off.

"Jonah!" I said a little too loudly.

He stopped, looking alarmed.

"Thanks."

He shook his head. "Don't thank me. I should have been more helpful from the start. Especially knowing how hard school is for you."

He disappeared from my screen. I danced around the room and then into the hallway to see if Oma was still here.

She'd be happy to hear the news.

CHAPTER 16

The next day, Jonah bugged me nonstop until I agreed to leave a message for the "humanitarian in training" guy.

Eric Williams called back right away. School was almost out for the summer, so we agreed to meet at his agency's office. I asked Melissa to be my travel partner.

A week later, we were perched on a narrow bench trying to keep our nerves under control. Eric worked in a musty Victorian home that had been turned into offices. The place buzzed with activity.

"Alia?"

A young man with a welcoming smile stood on the red-carpeted staircase. I raised my hand and then felt silly. We weren't in class. He met us at the bottom of the stairs. As we reached him, I froze. I'd been so worried about why we were meeting, I hadn't thought about what he would be like.

Now, I was face-to-face with a smart-looking guy with stunning blue eyes. He was a bit taller than me and had short bronze hair along with the shadow of a beard.

He shook our hands. "I'm Eric. You're Alia, and so you must be a friend," he said to Melissa.

"Friend and classmate," she said. "I'm Melissa."

"Excellent. I love meeting people from my home turf," he said.

He guided us into a space crammed with desks and chairs. Video screens tuned to different news shows covered one wall. The audio filled the room as background noise. Another wall had screens rotating through pictures and number charts.

"Thanks for meeting with us," I said. I fought to keep my voice from trembling.

"Absolutely," he said. "This is a very important issue, and I want to help."

I fished my notebook and pen out of my bag. I gave Melissa a warning look as she made googly eyes at me.

Eric turned toward her. "Now, Melissa, are you working

with Alia on this project? How much should I include you in this conversation?"

Even cynical, no-one-affects-me Melissa was caught off guard by his full gaze.

"I'm along for the ride," she stammered. "But I'll listen. Maybe I'll learn something."

I couldn't wait to tease her about that later. Eric gave her a warm smile and then turned to me.

"I think you did a great job on your paper. What I'm giving you will help fill the information gaps and prepare for a campaign. Okay?"

I shook myself loose from staring into his gorgeous eyes. "I keep waiting for someone to tell me I'm wrong. I'm not a very good student. How could I come up with this when no one smarter has?"

Eric waved his hands like he wanted to stop my thoughts. "I don't think it has anything to do with smarts, whatever that means. You have the right combination of fresh eyes, a good head, and a good heart. I think you're selling yourself short. And you're not actually alone. Others have the same concerns about what's happening with seniors. Connecting it to genocide warning signs is new and worth attention. In fact, this could be the defining issue of our generation," he added. "You should feel proud to be getting involved and helping."

He tapped and swiped on a video display to pull up a web page. It showed a map of the United States with dots sprinkled on it in various spots, some larger than others. He zoomed in on our state. Then he clicked on a dot to pop up a second window. It showed a location, date, and other information.

"A network of human rights groups is starting to track incidents involving the elderly. This heat map shows there have been 150 known incidents of violence or serious civil rights violations. That is just this year and in just this state."

"What kinds of violations?" I asked.

Eric navigated to a list of what the heat map tracked. It included times when the elderly had been refused medical treatment or even food. This was on top of times when the elderly were assaulted, harassed, or threatened.

I felt sucker punched. I pictured Oma being treated like this. Unbearable.

He closed out the map. "This is about early detection and action. I saw in your paper that you connected this to a firebreak. That's excellent. We need to make what's happening really visible to create a firebreak. You can see how your project will fit in."

"Alia said she's supposed to recruit other kids to help. How should we do that?" Melissa asked.

I leaned into her side, so grateful she used the word *we*.

Eric started bringing up more websites. "Let's look at examples from some information campaigns on other subjects. Then, how about we brainstorm ideas?"

My stomach did a somersault at the big smile he gave us. It wasn't just that he was drop-dead handsome. He was also sweet and smart and into saving the world. It made me want to be more like him.

But it hit me. I usually only focused on my latest tennis rankings for getting recruited for college. But if this was a glimpse into what I'd need to do in college classes, I certainly wasn't ready. Could I ever be ready for college? It seemed impossible. Should I focus on trying to go pro in tennis instead? What if I wasn't good enough for that either?

My thoughts swirled as we watched a ton of videos about different social causes. An hour later, I had a list of a gazillion agencies and readings. Eric had also drawn an example of how to create a plan. He called it mind mapping. It looked like a weird spider shape with circles and spindly lines.

We left with the promise to send him the plan and keep him involved. The sun spilled out from behind dark clouds as we made our way to the train for home.

"Don't even start with any crushing jokes," I warned Melissa, playfully pushing her forward. "He's a lot older and way out of my league."

"So?" she said. "Gets you thinking about the future after high school. Oh my god, gorgeous eyes. Absolutely gorgeous. I feel a song coming on."

I tolerated her belting out a random tune as we walked.

But on the train, the weight of sorting out my future and Oma's situation started stressing me.

"Knock it off," I snapped at Melissa as her singing got louder. I instantly felt bad. "I'm sorry. I just need to think. I can't pull this off. This is too much for me."

"You're right."

I waited for Melissa to dish out some spite because I'd hurt her feelings. Instead, she put her arm around my shoulder.

"But it isn't too much for a group of us. Let's work on it together. You'll be the leader so Mr. Carver gives you the extra credit."

I relaxed back into my seat. "Who cares about extra credit? This is much bigger than that."

I needed a small task to help get my panic under control. I took out my notebook. I drew a diagram like Eric showed us, listing out the different skills and knowledge we'd need. I knew to count on Melissa, Jonah, Wally, and Eric. Plus Oma and the Generativity group. Dad? Maybe. Mom? Doubtful.

How about Mr. Carver? I asked Oma if he was worried about his own parents. She said I should ask him myself. I would. And I had a good feeling we could get his help.

The number of circles and connecting lines grew in the diagram. I no longer felt so alone.

CHAPTER 17

The last days of school went fast. I scraped by in all of my classes. My "show them I'm serious" plan seemed to have helped. Mom and Dad took all the credit, of course, because of their academic probation threat.

I kept my starter position on the tennis team. And my national ranking was decent for going into my senior year. I was supposed to feel on top of the world about that. And also excited about going to a college prospect camp later this summer. But college didn't feel like a vague thing anymore. I'd have to commit to a next step within a few months. Pure panic ran through me every time that reality popped into my head.

It was good, in a not-good way, that I had the Generativity project to keep me distracted. Especially because things kept getting scarier with Oma. She'd been out of touch for a week now, sent to a mandatory Care

Camp. She'd promised to message me. Fear took over as no messages came through.

Tonight, we were starting work on a campaign. Mom and Dad didn't want to be a part of it. But they agreed everyone could come to our place if we kept our meetings low profile.

"Any ideas?" Wally waved a marker in front of his face.

"I know!" Melissa said, bouncing up and down on the couch. "How about Saving the Seniors?"

Jonah shook his head. "Sounds too much like Save the Whales. Or one of those other endangered species groups."

"Well, it kind of is like that," Melissa said. She shoved his leg with her hand.

"I'll write it up," Wally said. He scratched the marker across the big piece of paper taped to the wall. We only had three ideas listed so far. None seemed very good.

Ann joined Wally at the wall. "Let's play with it. Write up the key words you want to communicate. Things like *elderly* and *protect.* Then think of ways to connect them. Just toss out words."

Jonah said, "*Elderly* is good. So is *protect*. *Seniors*. *Safety*. *Civil rights*. *Freedom*. *Choices*. *Support*. What else?"

I had a thought. "We want this to be a group that grows. People should know they can join in and help out. What if we include *network* or *team* or *committee*?"

As Wally wrote up the words, the doorbell rang. My stomach grumbled loudly as the mouth-watering smell of pizza announced Mr. Carver.

"There are drinks and a salad in the car if you guys can get them," he said.

"How are you doing tonight, John?" Ann asked.

It was weird enough having my teacher in my house. It was beyond weird hearing him called by his first name.

After we all grabbed dinner, I directed Mr. Carver to our list on the wall. "We've been brainstorming a name for the group."

He studied the list. When I'd invited him over, I asked about his own family. His mother was already gone. His father was in a care center and had a low SSS. I'd stopped asking questions when his eyes got watery.

Now, he grabbed a marker and circled some words. Then he wrote out something on the paper. He stood back so we could see.

Elderly Protection Network.

"What if we add in the word *rights*?" I asked. "The Elderly Rights Protection Network."

"Sounds really official," Wally said.

"Alia, this started out as your project," Ann said. "I think you should have final say on the name."

Melissa held out her hand to Mr. Carver for the marker. She blocked the paper so we couldn't see while she wrote. Then she moved to the side with a "Ta-da!"

ERPN will crush CLEAR!

Everyone whooped and clapped.

"Okay, I guess we have a name," I said. "Wow."

By the end of the meeting, everyone had signed up for a project to help ERPN get started. But we had lots of questions to figure out, including how to recruit more students. I felt buried under the avalanche of too much information coming too fast. My face must have showed it. Wally came to the rescue.

"One step at a time, just like Mr. Carver said," he whispered. I gave him a fist bump.

"Before I forget," Ann said. "Let's keep John's—Mr. Carver's—involvement to ourselves. We don't want to jeopardize his job."

"Is that a risk?" Jonah asked. "Could you get in trouble?"

Mr. Carver shrugged. "It's a point of debate right now in the school district. Thank you, Ann. But I'm proud to be helping students think for themselves and take stands on social justice topics. Remember, my own father is being impacted by what's happening."

By the end of the meeting, I was exhausted. Still, I had one more thing to do before bed.

I video-called Eric and shared about ERPN.

"Great start!" he said. His grin made my heart skip.

"Thanks," I said. I breathed deeply to keep my emotions in check. "We're going to work on recruiting more kids."

"That's great, but . . . are you okay?" he asked. "You look tired or upset."

And with that, the tears were unleashed. "I'm worried about my grandma. She's at that Care Camp. I can't reach her."

"Ah, the camp," he said. "I'm sorry you're dealing with it directly. Can I ask what your grandma's score is?"

"She won't tell me exactly but says it's high." I imagined Oma giving the camp workers a run for their money. I worried they'd lower her score for being difficult. The lower the score, the less freedom she'd have.

"Well, it has to be high if she's enrolled in the camp," Eric said. "I don't know how else to say it. They wouldn't bother if her score fell below a certain level. But hopefully this gives you energy to keep going with the work you've started. We need to mobilize this summer. Okay?"

We agreed to check in again, then I headed to bed.

Eric's calmness rubbed off on me. It was the first good night's sleep I'd had in a while.

CHAPTER 18

It took a lot of brainstorming to figure out a recruitment strategy.

We wanted to stay off CLEAR's radar for now. That meant not posting flyers on the student bulletin board. Or doing blasts on our social channels. We had to go low-tech and low-key.

First, we divided up a list of kids we thought might feel the same way we did. Then, we came up with how we'd tell them about ERPN. We also thought through a response if they had any kind of negative reaction.

Reaching out to people felt nerve-racking. And we weren't always successful. In the first week, we got a few maybes and some nos. But at least no one had flipped out on us. Better yet, we snagged three students—Jake, Antonio, and Daria—who offered to recruit more people.

Jake was a friendly sophomore on the wrestling team

whose grandparents were in the same boat as Oma. Antonio did theater with Melissa and also had impressive tech skills. Daria was president of the Muslim-American Student Association. Like Jonah, she was a busy go-getter who commanded attention when she spoke. All three had jumped right in with ideas and offers to head up projects.

I was celebrating in my room and planning to make another round of calls when I got even better news. Oma was back from Care Camp! The kitchen was a loud, chaotic place as we all hugged Oma again and again. Finally, we gathered around the dinner table to hear about Oma's experience.

"I'm not supposed to talk about it," she said. "But, of course, I'll tell you everything."

We laughed. I was so relieved to have her back and to see that her attitude hadn't changed.

Everyone at camp had to surrender their cell phones, she explained. That's why she didn't keep us updated. Each day involved a series of activities.

"They gave me blood tests and body scans to see how

my organs and joints are working," she said. "Exercises to see if I'm frail. Tests to determine my cognitive functioning level."

"What's that?" I asked.

"How my brain is working," she explained.

"And?" Mom asked. "Did they give you some results?"

"An updated SSS," Oma said with disgust. "Like I already knew, I have a sharp mind and many years to live."

"So, no changes?" Dad asked.

"I'll stay in my current apartment at the care center," she said. "I'm supposed to feel lucky about that."

"I miss your house," Wally said.

Oma messed with his hair. "I do too."

"So, everything's okay?" Mom said. "The camp turned out okay?"

Oma stared at her intently. "Listen," she said. "Exercise routines, nutrition plans, and brain games are good for seniors. And some people need tips on how to stay connected to others to avoid loneliness. The problem is that people's freedoms are being taken away just because of their age. I didn't have a choice about going to Care Camp. I didn't have a choice about moving. They're taking away even more choices for others."

Mom grabbed Oma's hand tight. "I was reading yesterday about more violent attacks against elderly people. This wasn't what I'd pictured." She closed her eyes and sighed. "I agree that it's all going too far."

Relief washed over me as Mom admitted this. I hated how tense things had become between us.

During dinner, Wally and I filled in Oma about ERPN and how we were putting together a campaign. Our parents had stopped fighting against me speaking out. It still made them nervous, especially since Wally joined too. But I caught them throwing each other little smiles at times. Good smiles, like they were proud.

After dinner, Oma followed me to my room and closed the door.

"I want to be one of the faces of the ERPN campaign," she said.

"No way!" I shot out. "It's too dangerous."

"It is my duty to speak out," she said. "We must fight."

"We can do this without putting you in the spotlight," I pleaded. "If you anger the people in charge, they could lower your SSS. It's too risky. Can't you be behind the scenes guiding us?"

"I will do that, of course," she said. "But I think you need me out front too. An idea popped into my head during dinner."

She plopped down on my bed and got comfortable. I joined her and fought every anxious thought racing through my head as she shared what she wanted to do.

CHAPTER 19

A few weeks later, Oma and I stood at the edge of the living room and tried taking in what we could see. Our house had become ERPN Central and was filled with students. Today was the day everything had to come together into a real campaign.

"I can't believe this is actually happening," I told her.

"You pulled this off," she said. "You're my rock star."

The doorbell rang, interrupting my private moment with Oma. There stood Eric, looking extra casual in shorts and a vintage *We Are the World* T-shirt.

"Surprise!" He held up a canvas grocery bag. "Fuel for the troops."

I faked being calm. "Oh my gosh, I'm so glad you're here. There's so much to get done, and we really need a pro."

Oma joined others in the living room. Eric and I took

the snacks into the kitchen. Seeing him in person made me self-conscious all over again.

"Okay, Ms. President. Give me an assignment," he said.

I thought for a moment. "Maybe work with Wally to get teams ready to present?"

He headed off to find my brother.

An hour later, everyone was ready for a campaign run-through.

Eric pointed to a list on the wall. "Team leaders, come up here one by one and share your work. If you have questions for the group, please ask them."

Wally pointed to another sheet of paper. "I'll write up questions or suggestions."

I called up Jake and the Print Team first. He shared posters that showed seniors doing different activities. Some were serious; some were fun. Boldly colored text mixed with the photos: *They used to be our age. Someday, we'll be theirs. They deserve our respect. They can teach us a lot. No human life should be wasted.* At the bottom, text invited readers to join ERPN and stop the oppression.

"We thought showing a variety of seniors could help kids see someone they could relate to," Jake said.

The group whooped and clapped for the Print Team. Jake took a goofy bow on his way to sit down.

"Okay, let's hear from the Public Outreach Team next," I called out.

Melissa and Jonah came up.

"We've been working on two strategies," Jonah said. "One is having a lineup of speaking events. We've been putting together a list of blogs, podcasts, and community groups. We'll try getting some invitations to speak." He turned to Melissa. "Our second strategy was dreamed up by our resident drama queen. I mean that in the most flattering way. Melissa?"

Melissa clapped her hands with a grin.

"Okay, peeps. Just like with the printed materials, we want to remind people how much fun the elderly people in our lives can be. So, we're going to do a series of . . . drum roll please . . ." Melissa waited until some kids had started a fake drum roll. "Flash mobs!"

She raised her arms and waited for a reaction. She got a mixture of good-natured groans, claps, and whistles.

"I know you're thinking flash mobs are dead," she said. "But like good fashion, they come back in style. We're planning dance routines with all ages. We'll secretly spread the word of where and when each performance is going to happen."

A giggle escaped me as I pictured seniors getting their groove on.

"We do have a question for the group," Melissa said. "We've been thinking the dancers should end by tearing up SSS cards as a protest symbol."

This sparked quite the debate. Some people liked that it would remind people of the serious purpose. Others worried it could trigger anger and even put the dancers in danger.

We had a long discussion about different ways of protesting. Ann and Mr. Carver suggested we save this strategy to use later if the campaign wasn't producing the results we wanted.

I called up Antonio and the Web Team next. They projected our new website onto one of the walls, and the group cried out in excitement. Then, the room went silent as people looked over the details.

The website was simple but colorful and inviting. Links took visitors to pages with resources and important people to contact. Another link led to the map Eric had showed that tracked incidents.

"Oh, and every time someone joins our network, you'll see this ticker move and you'll hear this," Antonio said. He clicked a button. A pleasant chime rang out, like the sound of a Tibetan singing bowl.

"Ahhhhh," someone said. "Very peaceful."

"Nice choice," another student said.

I stared at the new ERPN logo on the website. It made us look so official. I worried about whether we could live up to the image.

The room was too quiet.

Ann piped up, "What are you all thinking right now?"

A sophomore named Miranda spoke. "The website looks great. I'm just sorting out in my mind that we're seriously going to do this. It looks so real. Just a bit nervous, I guess."

Others admitted they felt the same.

"It is serious," Ann said. "But I don't want you to be scared. We're all in this together. That's the power of numbers. And not doing anything would be scarier. Let's try to remember that. Okay?" She gave us a reassuring smile.

"Okay," I said. "Public Service Announcement Team, take us home with the final strategy. Oh, and let's give props to the Web Team!"

Applause broke out while Antonio sat down. Daria, the PSA Team leader, took her place at the front.

"This is the first in a series of videos," she said. "We want to see how people react before we finish the next."

I shot Oma a look. This was the idea she'd had about how to help.

The screen showed Oma and I sitting side by side, our arms touching. We were dressed in black against a white background.

"I'm Alia, and this is my oma," I told the camera, before looking over and smiling at Oma. "That's German for *grandmother*. My oma is a strong, smart, compassionate citizen of the world."

In the video, I took her hand. "She has taught me and my brother so much. We're not finished learning from her. And she's not finished teaching us or living her life."

I looked back at the camera. "Freedom doesn't have an age limit. Say thanks to the seniors in your life, and join us to make sure their rights are protected."

The video of us faded away. Then a slide came up with ERPN's contact information. Then that also faded to black.

The room was silent. I couldn't look at anyone, out of fear they didn't like it and fear that I'd start bawling.

Daria scanned the room. "Well?"

"Still stressed," said a friend of Wally's. "It's so freaking good, and so freaking real."

Others murmured their agreement.

"Ellen and Alia, you are wonderful," Eric said. "This takes a lot of courage. Thank you for stepping up. But remember that you won't be alone. PSA Team, I think you can interpret the silence as meaning this is excellent work."

The room erupted in applause. I smiled, trying to manage the panic rumbling inside.

Ann came to the front of the room to describe how things would roll out over the next few days. Afterward, people hung around to keep working on their projects.

Oma came over to me. "Okay?" she asked.

I nodded. I couldn't possibly put words to my confusing mixture of feelings right now.

Eric joined us. "I need to take off. Great, great work, Alia. How are you feeling?"

I could only shrug.

Oma smiled. "I'll let you two wrap up." She squeezed Eric's arm, then moved away.

"Listen," Eric said once she'd gone. "I know you're more worried than you want her to know."

I followed him out to the front yard. "What if this doesn't go great? What if we bring more trouble on ourselves, or people write us off?"

Eric pulled on his helmet. "It could happen. Remember the history cases you've studied. Rarely do people immediately see the need for change. If it were only that easy." He got on his bike. "So, you need to have thick skin. Don't start doubting yourself if our initial push is not well-received. Can you do that?"

I wanted him to believe that I could. I nodded.

"Well, I'm back to the city tomorrow, but you know I'll be helping. We'll check in, okay?" His smile made me want to go climb Mount Everest.

I watched Eric pedal away. I would keep his words close, like a good luck charm to keep me safe no matter what happened this week.

CHAPTER 20

A chime rang out. Followed by another. And then another. The chime went off every few minutes.

I was at the town's pizza joint with Jonah and Melissa. The number of members was growing faster than we'd ever expected.

It wasn't like this the day we launched. There were a few website hits, but mainly silence. I cried myself to sleep that night, convinced all of our hard work had been a waste of time.

But then people started passing around our flyers. The website hits started climbing. It looked like we were going viral.

"This is wild," Melissa said as chimes kept sounding from Jonah's tablet. He had it propped up against the napkin holder.

My phone buzzed. I answered fast when I saw it was Oma.

"I got a message from the PBS station," she said. "They want to interview us tomorrow. Both of us, together. What do you think?"

I didn't want to do it. But Jonah and Melissa thought I should. Jonah promised to help me prepare. I said yes, even though I wanted to say no.

"Courage, my dear," Oma said. "We have to keep up our courage. Your advisors there will help you prep in between mouthfuls of food."

The chimes kept coming while Jonah took me through likely interview questions. Melissa pretended to be her favorite PBS anchor. With typical Melissa flair, of course. She took on a deep, smooth voice and pinned me to my spot with an intense gaze while repeating Jonah's questions.

The next day, I met Oma at the Generativity office. We sat side by side for the remote interview. By then, our membership numbers were up to 300,000.

"This story is sure to prompt more people to sign up," Ann said to me. "How are you feeling?"

I couldn't lie. "Very nervous."

Oma's hand slipped into mine. "Remember, you're not alone. Now or ever."

I sucked in deep breaths to try staying calm. Suddenly, we saw a man on the computer screen. He introduced himself as the producer. He talked us through what would happen. Then, he counted down a ten-second warning.

Susan, the anchor, popped on our screen. I struggled to keep Melissa's anchor impression out of my head so I wouldn't burst into giggles.

Susan spoke. "And now we have two of the organizers behind this campaign here to tell us more about what prompted them to speak out. Alia Young and Ellen Berg, welcome."

My mouth was so dry I couldn't say thanks. I nodded and tried to smile.

"Thank you," Oma said in her velvety voice. She squeezed my hand outside the camera's view.

"Alia, I understand this started as a class project," Susan said. "Can you tell us more?"

Somehow, I stumbled my way through the story. How Mr. Carver's genocide homework had got me thinking about what was happening with elderly people. How Oma had helped me connect the dots.

I instantly regretted putting too much attention on her. But the interview was continuing.

Susan announced that the memberships of ERPN and Generativity were now up to a million combined. She asked for our thoughts. I couldn't say anything, I was so stunned.

"Alia? Any reaction?" Susan asked.

"Wow. It's really that high?" I asked.

"Do you think this confirms your theory? Clearly, you're not alone in being concerned," Susan said.

"No, I guess I'm not," I said.

"Susan, I'd like to ask anyone watching who hasn't signed up yet to join. Help us fight these oppressive laws," Oma said. "There are more reasonable ways to cope with the aging population. Let's all work together on this."

Susan thanked us for our time. Then she disappeared, and the producer came back on.

"Thanks so much. You both did a great job. Very well-spoken. And you didn't fidget too much!" he said.

We both laughed in relief and thanked him for getting us on the show. Once we'd disconnected, Oma and I hugged. "You were wonderful," she said, squeezing me hard.

"Oh my god, I was so nervous," I told her. "Was my voice shaking?"

She laughed and shook her head. "You looked cool as a cucumber."

My phone buzzed with a message from Melissa. *Way to rock it! The website is chiming nonstop. Woo-hoo!*

My phone blew up with more messages. Jonah, my parents, my brother, Eric, Mr. Carver. They all congratulated me. I felt like throwing up from the mix of excitement and nerves. I hugged Oma goodbye and headed home. I really needed to get in a tennis practice round. But I decided to skip it. I wanted to be back in my own space to deal with all of this. Plus, I couldn't risk seeing Charlotte. I was trying to ignore her constant attempts to turn the team against me. But going public like this could push the tension from a slow burn to a raging fire.

I spent the night hanging out with Wally and my parents. We listened to the chimes and returned messages. Melissa was frantic getting ready for the first flash mob tomorrow.

I checked the incident map. People were posting more stories of elderly abuse or oppression. Some stories were very hard to read. About seniors being left alone without food or supplies. Or being turned away in stores and restaurants. Or not getting medical care because hospitals said they had to follow new government rules that meant treating seniors last. Some people commented anonymously, saying they had tried to challenge the rules but found themselves in trouble. They applauded ERPN's work and our bravery but were afraid to become official members. Still, we did have new sign-ups flowing in. And the campaign had people talking in the open about it all.

Late in the night, exhaustion forced me to stop scrolling. A smidge of hope snuck up. This wasn't going to be easy, but maybe we could stop things from getting worse after all.

CHAPTER 21

The next day, the flash mob did its routine during a busy time outside the mall. People loved it. The video went viral and had a million hits in no time.

Another news show asked to interview me along with Oma and Ann. We would be in a studio sitting at a table for half an hour with the host. Once again, I didn't want to do it. It would put a huge amount of attention on us. And it sent my public speaking fears off the charts.

Jonah joined the family as we debated the pros and cons. I decided to try embracing the challenge. I was competitive in sports, after all. This was me trying a new sport. I'd lean into the discussion the same way our coach taught us to lean into a match.

The next day, Oma, Ann, and I found our way to the station in the city. A producer briefed us on how the show would work. Then she escorted us to a round table in the brightly lit studio. The news host introduced himself as George. Then he turned to another man and woman who were already seated. He introduced them as Robert and Martha. They smiled and seemed nice. But I noticed Ann and Oma exchanging a concerned look.

Oma whispered to me, "Robert and Martha are both with CLEAR." I tried not to show my surprise as Oma turned to the host. "We apparently missed this detail in the invitation."

My heart thudded with panic. But Robert and Martha just smiled and shook my hand. Maybe it would be okay. The producer called for quiet and started a countdown. The program's opening music began, and George kicked things off.

He started with some basic questions about ERPN and CLEAR. I was sharing about how my school project led to me creating ERPN when Robert cut me off.

"How would you solve the population crisis, Alia?" he asked.

I took a deep breath. "We need to look at all government

programs to find money that can be used to help the growing number of aging people."

"Excuse me," Robert said in a sarcastic tone. "But that's a talking point you've been fed that means nothing. We're trying to work on practical solutions that actually protect elderly citizens. You're busy stirring up emotions without any real answers."

Ann tried to get a word in, but Martha cut her off.

"Alia, we know your heart is in a good place. But you're in way over your head with this 'movement,'" she said, putting air quotes around the word. "You're not exactly a stellar student."

The host put up his hand for them to stop. "Let's keep this civil. Why would you accuse her of not being a good student? She's taken an extra credit project and turned it into a campaign that went viral within days. People everywhere are asking important questions about what's going on."

"I don't like to make students look bad. But I think it's important to know who's behind this 'successful' campaign," Martha said, again using air quotes. "You've got a teen who's near academic probation. She's at risk of losing her choice place in school sports. All of her thoughts on this situation have been planted by her grandmother. A woman who is known for her radical activism and ways of skating around the rules. I just think we should call this what it is."

"Alia?" The host turned to me. "Anything to say?"

I couldn't say anything. I was frozen in place by Martha's mean words. The worst part was that they weren't actually lies.

The host turned to Oma. "Ellen, do you feel this is a fair characterization, of your granddaughter and yourself?"

I was used to Oma being calm and collected. So I was shocked at the look on her face. She was clearly seething with anger and fighting to keep it under control.

"No, George, I do not," Oma said. "I'm very disappointed that CLEAR's representatives would make such accusations. Yes, Alia and her fellow members of ERPN are young. They are still learning the ins and outs of government financing.

But there are many grown-ups who don't understand such things."

She smiled at me. I saw her composure coming back. "I think we should all be proud of these kids. They are willing to speak out for something that concerns them, even when they don't have all the answers."

Then she turned her attention directly to Robert and Martha. "And to share private information about a student without her permission is offensive and possibly illegal. I would suggest you don't have all the facts. How about you focus on what is happening with the elderly in this country, not making personal attacks on kids who are concerned."

From there, the host turned the conversation back to the issue. But the damage had been done. CLEAR had called me out as a stupid student who didn't know what she was talking about.

We drove home in silence.

Oma's hand on my knee interrupted my mental replay of the show. "Okay?"

"Not really," I admitted. "But I'll get there."

Ann and Oma dropped me off at my house. I found Mom and Dad in the kitchen, having a serious talk. Wally was on the couch, waiting for me.

"What's up?" I asked him in a low voice.

"Customers have been calling Dad. They're pulling their plumbing business because of our work," he whispered.

"No!"

He shushed me. "Sounds like we'll have to be even more careful with our money now."

Mom and Dad cut off their conversation and came to the living room.

"There's our girl!" Dad said in a falsely cheery voice. "Our news star."

Mom tried to smile, but the corners of her mouth twitched. Soon she gave up and showed her anger. "I'm calling CLEAR headquarters to complain. Those jerks."

"No, Mom. Don't do that," I said. "I'll have to learn to handle these things. I wasn't ready today, but now I know to expect a personal attack. It won't shock me so much."

Mom jolted with a sudden thought. "Where's Oma?"

The thinly hidden panic in her voice hit me like a gut punch. "She went to the Generativity office with Ann. Why?"

Mom shook her head. "I just don't like how this all feels. There were some threatening calls. Let's make sure she's safe."

Dad started to call Oma.

"She and Ann wanted to send out new messaging," I said. "They're worried about CLEAR getting more aggressive. Do you think CLEAR is behind the threats toward your business?"

Mom shot Wally a look. "You're not supposed to be snooping."

"We'd find out anyway, Mom. You should tell us everything," Wally said.

She plopped down next to him. "We expected fallout from this."

Dad hung up. "She's not answering. I'm going to head over there."

"Let's go," Mom said.

All of the fear I'd pushed down flooded back. "I'm going with you."

"No. You need to stay here. We'll call with an update as soon as we can," he said while dashing out the door with Mom.

I collapsed next to Wally and texted Oma.

"There's more bad news," Wally said. "I didn't want to say it in front of them."

I waited. Afraid to know, afraid to not know.

"Looks like Charlotte is spreading fake stuff about you."

I opened my social media feed. First thing I saw was a video clip she'd posted of me making a massive mistake in one of our matches. She included the comment: *Anyone else hear the rumor she may be off the team soon?*

Wow. Totally false. But it had hundreds of views already, with lots of hurtful posts. Some from strangers, but some from kids I knew. Charlotte responded to those, hinting she knew other bad things about me.

Could this affect my rankings? And my prospects of

getting college offers? I didn't know whether to react online or stay quiet.

This day couldn't get any worse.

My phone buzzed. Oma!

Jonah.

"Hey there," I answered. "I hoped you were Oma. She's not answering our calls. My dad's going to find her."

He didn't say anything.

"Why are you quiet?" I asked. A wave of queasiness passed through me.

"Sorry. Just taking it all in."

"And did you see what Charlotte's doing online?" I asked. "She's totally trashing me."

"We'll deal with that later. Have you looked at the campaign activity?"

I put him on speaker so Wally could listen.

"The tone of the latest posts is bad," Jonah continued. "And our numbers are starting to drop."

Wally pulled up our website.

Our feed was filling up with new kinds of comments.

Hateful, angry remarks. People saying they were skeptical. The commenters wanted more proof. Some ERPN members were posting back, defending our information. But now there were a flood of anti-ERPN posts.

The membership counter was going haywire. The numbers zigzagged back and forth between members dropping and joining. The counter chimed anytime there was movement. It didn't care which way the numbers were going.

Wally and I looked back and forth between the ERPN page, my social media feed, and each other. We'd heard of this happening to other campaigns. We couldn't believe it was happening to ours.

Our work was flaming out as fast as it caught fire. What if everyone abandoned our cause? And where was Oma?

CHAPTER 22

Wally and I tried to keep busy as we waited to hear from Mom and Dad.

A painful eternity later, Dad finally called.

"We're with Oma at the hospital," he said. "She was attacked outside the Generativity office."

Wally and I burst into tears.

"She's going to be okay," he rushed to explain.

"What happened?" I asked.

"Two men wearing masks shoved Ann aside and then punched and kicked Oma. They took off fast. Ann called 911 right away. I know this is hard to take in."

"Can we come to the hospital?" Wally asked.

"No, I want you to stay inside, doors locked," Dad answered. "They're going to discharge her. We'll be home as soon as we can."

It was the middle of the night when they got back.

Seeing Oma battered broke my heart. And unleashed a kind of anger I'd never felt before.

I cradled Oma's head in my lap as she slept on the sofa. My fingers combed gently through her silver hair. It felt surprisingly wiry, given how soft it looked. A faint line of blood seeped through the large bandage on her forehead.

Even though I was exhausted, I stayed at her side as morning came. She pretended irritation, begging me to give her a bit of a break. But I think she liked my clinginess. It didn't matter. I wasn't going to stop.

The doctors said she'd recover okay. Mom's nerves were beyond frayed. It didn't help when Oma said she wouldn't back down.

I helped her to the kitchen in the afternoon. We made a pot of tea and a light lunch.

"I know you don't want to back off, but you've got to," I said as she tried to chew little bits of sandwich. "You could get attacked again. And the government could make things harder on you."

"I understand," she said. "Still, I cannot back down."

"But if the government comes after you and you refuse their orders, what will they do to you?" I asked. "And don't tell me to not worry. Give me a straight answer."

She studied me for an eternity. "They could put me in jail. But that's not going to happen."

I'd asked for the truth. I tried to not break down as she confirmed what I'd feared. "Why not? How could you avoid it if others haven't been able to?"

She took my hand. "I'm not giving you all of the details. I don't want you to feel like you have to lie if it ever comes to that. All I'll say is that I would disappear first."

"Disappear?" My voice came out as a screech.

"I've lived a long life. I know a lot of people, in a lot of different places. I would be safe. That's what I want you to know. I was planning to put this in a note for you. But I feel better being able to talk about it with you directly."

I leaned in. "You can't disappear. No."

She kissed my forehead. "I wouldn't be the first, or the last. And I promise you that I'd be safe. Then, if things turned around, I'd be back."

She wiped the tears I couldn't keep from falling. "Can I tell Wally? Do Mom and Dad know?"

"Yes, your mom and dad know. No, you can't tell Wally. I have a letter ready for him. Just in case. And remember how incredibly proud I am of you. I was before all of this. Now my admiration is off the charts."

"How is Mom taking this?"

Tears crowded Oma's eyes. "I'm so proud of her too. She's learning not to be so afraid."

We stayed quiet for a long time, our foreheads touching. I didn't have any words left that described the deep hole being torn in my soul.

* * *

After the attack, ERPN rallied with more public service announcements and a new flash mob. Things still got worse.

CLEAR was very organized and extremely aggressive. They put out videos and posters with elderly citizens saying they liked the new policies taking care of them. They also encouraged people to visit ERPN's headquarters to talk about the issues. We learned they'd posted our home address when two people rang our doorbell. They bullied a confused Wally into letting them into our living room. Mom and Dad called the police. The cops said it wasn't against the law to share public information.

The doorbell started ringing so much we worked out a signal to know when friends or the ERPN group were visiting. After we found a threatening note, Dad installed security cameras. We had to be extra careful coming or going.

Dad lost more customers. People who said they disagreed with us completely. And people who whispered how they didn't want to get caught in the middle.

Next, CLEAR spread a story about me. It made it sound like I was a screwup who never studied and was clueless about how the world worked. I was just a convenient face for Generativity who knew nothing about the real issues. They used unflattering pictures of me and suggested I was a bad-tempered brat who had to get her way.

What bothered me most were the mean comments

people posted. I thought of the times I'd seen such stories, usually about celebrities. I'd never posted a remark, good or bad. But I'd laughed at such comments. Now I knew how it felt and how easy it was to twist the truth.

My family, Jonah, and Melissa threw lots of love my way. They reminded me daily that the people who mattered knew the truth. Eric added his voice. He reminded me that *I* knew the truth and that's what mattered the most.

Then we got the news about Oma. The government did lower her SSS. She'd have to move to more restrictive housing by the fall. This housing was meant for people who were really sick or not able to get around easily. The government also ordered her to do therapy to help her accept being in her "twilight" years. The letter blamed it on her recent "accident," saying it had hurt her health. But we knew it was punishment for speaking out.

I held Oma's gaze and tried to look brave as I silently accepted that the time for her to disappear had arrived.

CHAPTER 23

We kept up ERPN's campaign even though the harassment and hate continued. Our new messages didn't spread like the first ones. Our membership numbers stopped growing so fast. We'd complained about the constant chimes before. Now we listened for any chime.

Charlotte was determined to ruin my reputation in the tennis world. My coach warned Charlotte and her parents about the school policy for online bullying. That was supposed to make me feel supported. But a warning did nothing to stop it. She just got sneakier. I tried to avoid practicing when I knew she'd be at the courts. But some of my other teammates got nasty online too. That made practice depressing and awkward no matter when I went.

Mom did yoga with me and encouraged me to picture things turning out okay. Dad asked me to help him organize our research in a big box file. He wanted to document the history unfolding right before us. Wally kept pumping out new ideas for the campaign. Oma stayed close and steadied us all. I demanded to be kept in the loop about the forced move still looming.

Everyone babbled on about the need for courage. I just felt never-ending fear.

I was in the middle of another sleepless night when a call came in. Jonah.

My gut gripped tight. He would only call at this hour if something was wrong.

I flipped on my bedside lamp, wrapped myself in my top sheet, and pulled my tablet closer.

Jonah's face popped on the screen.

"Hey there," he said. "I figured you weren't sleeping. I couldn't keep the news in any longer."

"What's happened? What's wrong?" I asked, failing to stay calm.

"Nothing bad. Breathe," he said. "It's good news. Congressman Nell wants to meet with us."

I was too exhausted and ready for scary news to

understand his point. "Who? Now? It's the middle of the night."

"Not right now, Alia," he said, chuckling. "I guess you *are* wiped. Nell is interested in what ERPN and Generativity are doing. He might go public opposing the elderly policies before Congress goes back in session."

He stared at me, waiting for a reaction. I didn't know how to react.

"Why aren't you cheering?" he huffed. "I've been working on this connection all summer."

"Sorry. I'm waiting for the part where you tell me there's a catch. Or a condition. Or a reason to not get too excited," I said. "Every time something good starts to happen, something bad follows. Why should this be any different?"

Jonah shrugged. "Somehow, I think it will be. I have a good feeling about this. You've been taking hard hits, Alia. Your family too. This meeting could be a turning point in our favor."

I brought my tablet in even closer so I could be eye to

eye with him. "Then you go meet with him. Let's pick the smartest people from our campaign. Not me. Making me such a public face in this has not worked in our favor. Let's change our luck."

He shook his head. "No way. My contact in his office says Nell feels bad about the way you're being treated. He wants to meet you and others from the core team. I hope you'll count me as part of your core team."

That made me laugh. Me getting to decide if Jonah should be part of my team to meet an elected official.

"It's good to see you smile," Jonah said.

"There's not a lot to smile about these days," I said, laying my head back on my pillow and resting the tablet nearby. "I'm so tired, Jonah. And so worried about Oma and my parents."

"There will be more to smile about soon. I hope this news helps. Promise me you'll try to sleep."

I smiled again. "Promise. I feel more relaxed already. I'm glad you let me know."

A few days later, I went back to the city with Jonah,

Ann, and Oma. We met Congressman Nell in his office. He reminded me of Mr. Carver—no nonsense but with a good heart. Going in, I could barely open my mouth. I felt ready to collapse with fright. By the end, though, I was talking about my tennis plans with him. He sent us on our way with icy water bottles to cope with the summer heat.

A week after that, Congressman Nell appeared on the same news show where we'd been ambushed by CLEAR. He asked the public to calmly explore the issue of how our country was handling the aging population. He planned to vote against the new geographic zones.

I didn't understand everything they discussed on the show. But the congressman kept saying how important it was to preserve the freedoms of seniors. I held on to that.

When the host asked him about my genocide theory, the congressman didn't shy away. He agreed it sounded far-fetched to many people. Then he pulled out the list of early warning signs Mr. Carver had given us for class. He read through it. He asked the host to help him evaluate the situation. They even pulled up the incident map and used examples from that.

"I know there were good intentions when the Senior Situation Score was first developed," the congressman told the host. "But we need to make sure this doesn't become a runaway train. And that groups don't have uncontrolled power deciding who lives and who dies."

He was the first national politician to go on record with concerns. He wasn't the last. Two more lawmakers joined the cry for a new review. Then three more added their voices.

Dad called it the pebble in the pond that could create ever-spreading ripples.

CHAPTER 24

The mood turned again. More people spoke out against the elderly laws. It became a top news story every day.

Now Ann and I were in another TV studio, going on another talk show. Robert and Martha from CLEAR were there too. We expected them to launch another personal attack against me. I wasn't looking forward to it, but I felt ready this time.

The producer gave the countdown. Keisha, the news host, kicked off the show.

Sure as fireworks on the Fourth of July, the CLEAR reps zeroed in on me within a few minutes. Keisha had asked for their reaction to ERPN's success over the summer.

"We all know that things can go viral even if they aren't the truth," Martha said. "Has ERPN gotten a lot of attention? Yes. Does that mean their views are accurate? No."

Robert looked at me as he spoke. "And with all due

respect, the group's leader is on the same shaky ground she was a couple of months ago. Maybe even in worse shape, based on what we're hearing."

I took a deep breath and put my hand out to stop the host from jumping in.

"ERPN is led by several students," I started. "Not just me. And I'm actually doing great personally. Despite everything going on, including the continued harassment of my family."

I looked directly at Martha. "You just said viral information isn't always accurate. I agree with you. I'd suggest you take that to heart when it comes to nasty rumors and personal attacks being spread by your followers."

Keisha gave me an admiring nod. Then she turned the discussion to the proposed laws. Ann jumped in to the debate about those. But I listened carefully and stayed on my guard until the show wrapped up and we were on our way home.

After that show, our chime rate increased again. Slower

and steadier than before. But the numbers went the right way. We vowed to appreciate each chime as a step toward change for the better. Eric sent me a message with one word: *Firebreak!*

My body had run on adrenaline for weeks. Relief sent me into a full energy crash. My parents ordered me to bed to recover. Wally found excuses to stop by my room. I acted irritated, and he acted clueless. But we both knew things were good between us.

No one besides Oma knew just how big my relief was. Congressman Nell described her as a courageous senior facing violence and backlash for telling her story. That prompted the government to suddenly improve her status. She wouldn't need to move for now. Or disappear.

"I'll stay and fight," she said each time I asked her about her plans.

Support for a law moving the elderly into zones seemed to be fading. But we weren't out of the woods, as Dad loved to say. None of the other elderly policies had changed yet, after all. CLEAR was still stirring things up. Dangerous things were still happening.

Charlotte was on the courts the day I jumped back in to my practice routine. We hadn't talked face-to-face all summer. At least she'd stopped posting about me. Maybe she was changing her tune, maybe not. We kept our distance and ignored each other.

The weirdness would be there when school started again. With Charlotte and with others. Had this issue divided us forever, or could we fix the cracks?

For now, I focused on my play. The tennis ball took the force of my complicated feelings. I vowed to keep up my confidence, on and off the court.

CHAPTER 25

ERPN and Generativity organized an end-of-summer potluck.

My stomach went into hungry mode when I walked into the meeting hall with Wally, my parents, and Oma.

I slipped a little box into Ann's hand with a smile. She unwrapped it and pulled out a charm bracelet with different symbols of peace.

"Alia, this is beautiful," she said, hugging me.

"There she is." Melissa's arms wrapped around me from behind. Jonah came to my side.

"So much has happened since spring," Ann said to me. "To be honest, I didn't know if you would stick with it when you first showed up at our meeting. You seemed so scared and overwhelmed. Look at you now."

She and my friends beamed at me, and I felt a glow of pride. Another voice interrupted the admiration fest.

"Here are my favorite activists." Eric held a large salad.

"Oh, I like the sound of that. Activist," Melissa said. "I feel a new song coming on."

Jonah and I groaned, but others around us encouraged her to sing. Melissa made everyone laugh with an over-the-top Broadway-style tune about activism.

"Dinner!" someone called. People swarmed the food. It had been a long, stressful summer. The stress wasn't going away. But this was a nice chance to take a break and recharge. I decided to enjoy the feast.

"Alia, come with me," Oma said as I studied the desserts.

People had gathered in a half circle. Oma gently parted them to bring us to the center. The room quieted down.

Uh-oh. Something really embarrassing was about to happen.

"We want to recognize everyone's efforts this summer." Oma smiled. "Starting with my granddaughter."

She looked at Mr. Carver, and he took over. "You've all heard how Alia got involved in this movement. It started with the genocide unit in my class. I couldn't tell her about

Generativity at the time. Instead, I offered her an extra credit project."

I didn't know how to stand or look as everyone stared at me. My face grew hot. I felt a poke in my back and heard Wally whisper, "Deep breaths."

Mr. Carver gave me a big smile. "You've more than earned your extra credit. Keep up the good work, Alia."

The group gave me a round of applause. People whooped and cried, "Way to go, Alia!"

I shook Mr. Carver's hand and turned to fade back into the group. He held tight to keep me there.

"Not so fast," he said as people chuckled.

Ann stepped forward, dragging a big bag with her.

"We know you were motivated by much more than extra credit," she told me. "You recruited some fabulous helpers, formed ERPN, and created an amazing campaign. The Generativity members chipped in a little money to give your crew a new look."

She pulled out a T-shirt sporting our ERPN logo in colorful letters. It was beautiful.

Soon, the core ERPN team all wore the new T-shirts. Cameras snapped away at our smiling lineup. We had all learned and worried together.

I still hated speaking in public, but I fought down my nervousness. I waved my hands to quiet the group.

"I'd like to say one thing." I grabbed my parents and Oma. "All of the grown-ups here have been a huge help. And taken big risks. But I really need to thank my parents. They let our home become a headquarters and have suffered because of it. And I don't have the right words to thank my grandma. I'd like to have one small fraction of her strength."

I had to stop there. My emotions threatened to take over. Oma squeezed me hard as people clapped.

The group broke up. Eric appeared at my side while Wally and I admired our new shirts.

"I'm going to say this in front of your family in the spirit of being completely open. I'm on a recruiting mission," Eric said. "I hope you'll consider the college information I sent you."

"Oh? Say more," my dad said. He really liked Eric.

"The school has a lot of different programs. Global studies, peace and conflict studies, international relations, as examples," Eric explained. "I think Alia has found a passion. This could be a good direction for her." He gave me that look that invited complete honesty. "Am I right?"

This was crunch time. I headed to prospect camp this weekend to show my tennis skills to college coaches. The idea of college did excite me for the first time. And it terrified me.

"Yes," I admitted. "But who knows if I could even get accepted into this college. You all know how hard school is for me. That hasn't magically changed."

"Colleges help students with learning disabilities," Mom said. "You'll get support."

"You did some pretty solid research to create the paper that led to ERPN, which led to today," Eric said. "How did you accomplish that?"

I remembered how lost I had felt. I looked at my little brother. I needed to suck it up and give him public credit.

"I tapped into Wally's brainpower. That got me going on a plan."

Wally puffed up with importance.

"Don't get a big head," I warned.

My parents smiled at me. I knew they were now a team, determined to encourage me.

"I think you're selling yourself short," Dad said.

Mom hugged me for the millionth time today. "Your quick instincts get you through a lot."

"At least tell me you'll consider it," Eric said.

How could I not promise this? Oma and other seniors weren't safe yet. And there were so many other groups of people in the world who weren't safe.

I nodded my promise. To all of them. And to myself.

This project had opened my eyes to a lot. Some of what was going on in the world was very scary. But it felt reassuring to have solid ideas about my future for the first time. I didn't know where I'd end up after high school. But I couldn't wait to start figuring it out.

ABOUT THE AUTHOR

Jennifer Phillips writes stories that celebrate creativity, courage, and determination. She started out as a newspaper reporter in the Midwest and then spent many years in corporate and nonprofit communications. Now she splits her professional energy between writing for children and helping grown-ups make things work better through process improvement and creativity methods. She also advocates for social justice needs, especially concerning disability and mental illness. A Seattle mom of two young adult girls and one bird, she has more story ideas than time. She does her best writing super early in the morning when the coffee is piping hot and the house extremely quiet. *Firebreak* is her seventh book for children and teens. Come visit her at jenniferphillipsauthor.com.